A
Harlequin
Romance

OTHER
Harlequin Romances
by HILDA PRESSLEY

Many of these titles are available at your local bookseller,
or·through the Harlequin Reader Service.

For a free catalogue listing all available Harlequin Romances,
send your name and address to:

HARLEQUIN READER SERVICE,
M.P.O. Box 707, Niagara Falls, N.Y. 14302
Canadian address: Stratford, Ontario, Canada.

or use order coupon at back of book.

WHEN WINTER
HAS GONE

by

HILDA PRESSLEY

HARLEQUIN BOOKS   TORONTO
WINNIPEG

Original hard cover edition published in 1974
by Mills & Boon Limited.

SBN 373-01821-5

Harlequin edition published October 1974

CHAPTER ONE

IT all began one dreary February afternoon, darkness gathering rapidly. Marlene had never been so unhappy in her whole life. The warmth of the huge glasshouse could do nothing to warm the ice around her heart, and for the first time in her life the exotic beauty of the plants and flowers failed to stir her. The weather outside more nearly matched her feelings —cold, damp and gloomy with fog beginning to develop as the afternoon hurried prematurely to meet the winter evening.

So it was when she tried to see into the future. In spite of having a job she loved, she could see nothing through the cold mist of her thoughts except gloom and despair. The two people who had meant most to her, on whom her life's happiness depended, had become lost to her. Roger, whom she had hoped to marry, was going to marry someone else. Her father whom she had loved dearly had died suddenly of a heart attack. He had been her only parent and she had neither brothers nor sisters.

Both events had happened so unexpectedly. She had thought Roger loved her as much as she had loved him. Over and over again he had vowed he loved her, had talked of marriage. Heir as he was to this great house and estate, to some their affair had seemed remarkable, but to others perfectly natural and in tune with the times. For her father had been head gardener here. Highly skilled and qualified with a great deal of responsibility and many men working under him, he had nonetheless been an employee, and so had she—still was, and responsible for all the house plants and special flowers used to decorate the great house. The difference in their social standing had appeared to mean nothing to Roger. But quite without warning he had decided that it was his 'duty' to marry the daughter of a neighbouring wealthy landowner.

"We need the money, you see, sweetheart. I owe it to the family," he had said. And what had hurt most of all: "It needn't make any difference to you and me. At least, not so very much. We can still see each other. Nothing easier these days—"

Marlene closed her eyes in an effort to shut out the memory. She no longer loved him. How could she? He had shown a side of himself she could not possibly love. But it would be a long time before she would love again. Her pride, and her faith in her own judgement of people, had suffered a very severe blow indeed. And a few weeks after Roger's engagement had been announced her father had collapsed and died of a coronary thrombosis.

Deep in the gloom of her thoughts, she did not at first see the tall stranger who stood for a few moments regarding her. She turned to give her attention to a rubber plant whose main stem had been broken by a careless cleaning woman up at the house. It was then she saw him. He looked foreign, she decided—dark-haired, very formally dressed in a dark suit and an immaculate white silk shirt, his skin bronzed by a sun much more warm and constant than their own.

She opened the glass door of the greenhouse. "Can I help you?"

He eyed her gravely for a moment or two, then gave a faint smile.

"I was given permission by Lord Hetherington to look around his glasshouses. He told me I would find

6

you somewhere about. May I come in?"

"Of course." She opened the door wider and stepped aside to allow him to enter.

"Thank you. Most kind," he said with the marked courtesy also of a foreigner, but in perfect English. "Permit me to introduce myself. My name is Juan de Montserrat. I come from Spain—from what might be called a fishing village called Blanes." He paused and eyed her expectantly.

"I—I'm afraid I've never been to Spain, and I've never heard of it," Marlene answered apologetically.

"Do not worry. Though many people visit Blanes we have so far resisted the temptation to build large four- or five-storey hotels. It is not really a village. It is a port, but one of its main industries is fishing. Indeed it is renowned for its fish market on the quay. It is situated on that part of the Spanish coast known as the Costa Brava, or wild coast, not really very far from Barcelona."

"I see."

Not a very intelligent reply, but his appearance had been so sudden and had so jerked her out of her thoughts, she was feeling like someone who has just awakened from a deep sleep. Moreover, she found his presence rather overwhelming. He gave the impression of being a man of some substance and importance, and at the same time there was something unusual about him which she could not quite pinpoint.

He seemed quite unaware, however, of any impression he might be making. He was gazing around at the plants and flowers with a great deal of interest.

"Tell me, do you know all the names of these plants?"

"Of course."

"And how to cultivate them?"

"Naturally. It's my job."

7

"Fascinating. Quite fascinating."

He went from one plant to another asking questions about their propagation, their likes and dislikes with what seemed to be genuine interest. Marlene answered him, wondering why he was here, whether he was a friend of Lord Hetherington. Then his attention was caught by the broken rubber plant.

"Ah! And what has happened here?" When Marlene told him he asked: "What will you do with it?"

"I shall try to propagate a new plant."

"How will you do that?"

"Well, I shall make a careful slit into the stem about here, some four inches long—" she pointed to a suitable section "—and insert some damp spaghnum moss, then wrap the whole thing in polythene and tie it top and bottom. Within a few weeks it should have formed new roots."

"Fascinating," he said again. "You must love plants very much indeed."

"Yes, I do." She asked him if he would like to see her special greenhouse. "I call it my hothouse. I have plants and flowers in there which need a warmer, more humid atmosphere than those in here."

"I'd be delighted."

She led the way to a smaller greenhouse a few yards away, and almost before they entered he gave exclamations of delight.

"Ah yes! Well now—"

Marlene closed the door against the cold air outside and stood there for a moment wtih conscious pride as he went from one rare and exotic plant to another. All she had grown from either cuttings or seeds or from division, and any plants which did not quite measure up to her own and her father's high standard were ruthlessly discarded. In particular she

8

was proud of her orchids and the Bird of Paradise. The strelitzia, which looked exactly like the head of a scarlet bird, she had grown from seed and nurtured for four years before being rewarded with their exotic blooms.

Her visitor ran his finger gently along the 'beak' and head plumes. "Beautiful," he murmured, "beautiful," in a voice almost like that of a man who was caressing the woman he loved. He turned and looked at her. "In the Carl Faust botanical garden in Blanes the Bird of Paradise grows out of doors."

Her eyes widened with interest. "Really? How wonderful!"

"Yes, it is." Then he said suddenly: "Miss Sheridan—"

Marlene started. She did not even realize he knew her name. "Yes?" she enquired, as he paused.

"I wonder—will you do me a great favour?"

"Why, of course," she answered, thinking perhaps he was about to ask her for a cutting of a plant or a seedling. But she was totally unprepared for what he did ask of her.

"Will you have dinner with me tonight? At my hotel."

She gave him a startled look. "I—I don't know."

"A prior engagement, perhaps?" he queried.

"No, not really, but—"

His invitation had taken her completely by surprise. Why should he ask her? They had only met about half an hour ago and he did not look the kind of man who went around dating women on such short acquaintance. He was a dignified, rather than a romantic figure.

"I ask you for two reasons," he said, as if reading her thoughts. "First, I hate dining alone—especially in a strange hotel, and second, I have a proposition

9

to put to you."

"A proposition?" she repeated.

"Yes, but please do not ask me to tell you now. A long explanation is necessary, and I would prefer to do it at leisure over a meal, if you would be kind enough to accept."

Now she was intrigued, and she was finding his formality and old-fashioned courtesy quite pleasing. She hadn't been taken out anywhere by anyone since—

She broke off her thoughts abruptly and accepted his invitation.

"Good," he said in a businesslike tone. "Then I shall call for you at six-thirty."

Marlene told him where she lived—which was in one of the cottages on the estate—and he departed. Within seconds he had become swallowed up in the mist, and she began to wonder if he had been a figment of her imagination.

She went back to the other greenhouse and rendered a form of botanical first aid on the rubber plant, then made her way to the cottage. It was old with a wealth of oak beams and low ceilings modernized to the extent of central heating, hot and cold water and electricity, and was nicely decorated, yet tonight it seemed more lonely than ever. The clocks ticked too loudly in the great silence and everywhere she looked she was reminded of her father—his chair, the many items of antique furniture he had collected from time to time, his pipe rack, his books.

She switched on television and listened to the news while she made a cup of tea. She was glad to be going out this evening. The long winter months still to come were going to be pretty well unbearable.

She took some time deciding what to wear for her dinner engagement with Mr Juan de Montserrat—or should she call him Señor? He would most certainly wear a dinner jacket, she guessed, and he would like a woman to dress quietly yet with style. She chose a long black velvet dress she had not worn for some time, set off by a double string of pearls, a Christmas gift from her father. All she could do about her blonde hair was brush it and pile it up. She was applying a last-minute touch to her make-up when the door bell rang—at exactly one minute past the half hour.

She opened the door to him and he stepped inside for a moment.

"You are very prompt," he told her as he took in her appearance. "And you look—charming, if I may say so."

"Thank you. May I offer you a drink before we go?"

Her supply of drinks was modest, but there still remained part of a bottle of her father's favourite drink she could offer him.

"Thank you, yes," he said, his glance flitting around the room. "This is perfectly delightful. I've heard much about the English cottage, but this is the first time I have actually been inside one."

She handed him his drink and poured out a small sherry for herself.

"It—doesn't actually belong to us—to me. It's part of the estate," she told him.

"But the furniture and so on are yours, are they not?"

She nodded. "My father's hobby was collecting antiques, especially furniture. His—study and the upstairs rooms are full of them."

"And did you share his enthusiasm?"

"To some extent, yes."

She noticed that he did not ask her about her father, and came to the conclusion that Lord

Hetherington or someone must have told him.

He drove them to his hotel in his own car which he had brought from Spain. It was very smart and luxurious in the extreme. Marlene guessed he must be a very rich man. He certainly seemed well accustomed to having the best of everything, knew what he wanted and how to get it. The way he ordered the meal and the wine gave evidence. Roger had always had a good command of himself, but this man displayed an authority with a lift of his finger.

She waited to hear what his proposal was, but during the meal he talked about Spain, its customs, its turbulent history. He spoke with pride and affection of 'my country' and 'our people'.

"Were you born in Blanes?" she asked him.

He shook his head, but did not volunteer any further information about either his birth or his parents.

"Let us now talk about you," he said. "I sense that you are not very happy. Indeed, if you will forgive my saying so, you looked most *un*happy when I first saw you through the windows of your greenhouse. You did not at first see me, I think."

At this Marlene told him about the death of her father and how much they had meant to each other. She did not want to talk about Roger.

"And at the moment you are living alone in your cottage?" he queried, after expressing his sympathy for her loss. "Surely it is not good for you to be alone?"

"I suppose not, but one becomes accustomed to these changes of circumstance."

He shook his head slowly. "No one should have to get accustomed to living alone—or allow themselves to if they can help it. I've heard people say that they would rather live alone than live with someone they cannot get along with. But learning to 'get along' with others is a part of life." Then, abruptly : "As we have finished our meal, shall we retire to the lounge for coffee and continue our conversation there?"

She agreed, thinking over what he had just said. He was a man with a philosophy evidently. He was right when he said that one should not live alone. The cottage when shared with her father had seemed, at times, on the small side, especially when they had friends in. Now, it appeared over-large as well as silent and empty. She could well imagine how the personalities on television in the regular series programmes could become a very real part of life—a lonely, artificial life. But what could she do? She did not know anyone who would share the cottage with her, and in any case she had been feeling too grief-stricken and dispirited to make an effort about anything except her job and keeping the cottage in order. Would she, really, become accustomed to it and join the community of people who became part of the artificial life of the small screen? The idea appalled her and yet she did not feel she had the mental energy to do anything about it.

Juan de Montserrat waited until they had been served with their coffee before he spoke again, and he then came directly to his proposal.

"Miss Sheridan, I wonder—would you consider an offer of a post in Blanes—working for me?"

Her eyes widened swiftly. Whatever else she had expected it had not been this.

"What—what kind of post?" she temporized, wanting time to think.

"Doing roughly the same kind of thing you are doing now. Caring for plants."

"You—you're not, by any chance, connected with those botanical gardens you were telling me about?"

13

He shook his head. "I'm afraid not. Something far more mundane. I own several hotels in the area—two in Blanes, others in various places along the coast."

"But what possible caring for plants can there be in hotels except simply watering them?" she asked in astonishment.

"You'd be surprised. Of course I realize that such a job might not be quite what you've been accustomed to—although I had it in mind to buy a small glasshouse. On the other hand, you would probably find more scope than you think. In my hotels in Blanes I have paved gardens where the guests like to sit for aperitifs, for instance, or in the evenings. At my hotel in Pineda, a charming village further along the coast, there is actually a garden with trees and shrubs and a small lawn. I would still pay a man to cut the lawns, of course, as I do now," he said swiftly. "Er—and he would still do the weeding."

Marlene could not help smiling. "And what would I be expected to do except water the plants?"

"Care for them generally, replace them when they have passed their best, choose the right kind of plants for the sun or shade. That sort of thing—and more perhaps."

"But who is doing all this at present?"

"Various people. At Pineda, the outdoor plants and shrubs by the gardener, the indoor ones by a porter. At Blanes, the job is shared by my assistant and the waiters. Most unsatisfactory to all concerned. The flowers and plants are provided—and often chosen—by the local florists and nurserymen, but neither the gardens at Pineda nor the paved gardens at Blanes are as colourful and as well looked after as I would like."

Marlene found herself sympathizing with his problem, sharing his regret that the plants needed better care and even wanted to do something about it. But

14

caution put a brake on her feelings. What was she about? How could she leave her job here, uproot herself to go to another country—and work in hotels? The idea was too absurd.

She shook her head swiftly before she had time to weaken again. "No, no. I'm sorry, but I can't. It's out of the question."

His face showed neither surprise nor regret. He simply eyed her in silence for a moment.

"You are perhaps engaged to be married?"

"No," she answered sharply, "I'm not."

He shrugged. "In that case what is there to keep you here? Even if you found you did not like it in Spain, you could always return, though I would hope you will not, naturally. I imagine someone with your talent and qualifications could soon find another post —or even come back here."

Come back here? All at once she wanted nothing more than to get away.

Juan de Montserrat pressed his advantage. "Why not give it a trial for six months or a year? You can have a small flat overlooking the bay at Blanes—and I can assure you that bay is quite something. You would have ample scope for your talents and full responsibility. Also whatever salary you are receiving here, that you can have—and more."

"But—but why?" she demanded uncertainly.

"You may find you need more money in a foreign country."

"I didn't mean that. I mean why me? Why come to England when you could doubtless find someone in your own country. A man, for instance."

"As to that, I fancy women have more flair for this sort of thing, more artistic sense. I did not actually come to England to find someone to care for my plants. I came for some other purpose. But when I

15

saw your work—well, I was very impressed." He paused, then said, "I have some photographs in my room. Suppose I go and get them to show you, and while I am away perhaps you could be thinking things over."

She hardly needed to think things over. She knew even as his tall, lithe figure crossed the room to the door that she would go. It seemed inevitable and so right, the perfect answer to her unhappiness. In Spain she would be far, far away from here on the day of Roger's wedding. Already her vision of a bleak future was fading. In its place she could see blue skies and a blue sea—the bay described by Juan de Montserrat.

Two days later she was already there, marvelling—when she had a moment to think and get back her breath—at the speed with which her life had suddenly changed.

Juan had arranged everything. As he had said, he had his car here. She might just as well go back with him. It would be so simple.

"But—but what about my job—and the cottage? All my father's antiques?" she had asked.

"They can be put into store until you decide whether or not you'd like them with you," he said easily. "As to your job, I'll see Lord Hetherington, if you like. After all, if you went on holiday or took ill suddenly, they would have to find someone else."

She argued no longer. Oddly enough, all at once none of it seemed to matter, except perhaps her father's treasured antiques. Blanes beckoned and she was only too willing to be gone.

Juan de Montserrat was at her cottage the following morning almost before she had finished breakfast. Somewhat bewildered, she invited him in.

"I thought you might need some help with your packing," he said. "I've had a word with Lord

Hetherington and he is quite happy about your going. He is going to miss you, of course, but for your sake he feels a change is the very best thing for you."

And to confirm this Lord Hetherington himself paid her a visit a few hours later, assuring her that whenever she felt she wanted to return her services would most certainly be needed.

It was Montserrat himself who arranged for a firm to collect her father's pieces of furniture and other antiques to put into store. He also supervised the handling and insisted on paying for six months' storage in advance.

"At the end of that time," he told her, "I hope you will feel settled enough to have it shipped out to Spain."

For the rest of the day she had difficulty in keeping pace with him as he helped to pack her books and other personal items she wanted to take with her.

"You will want to say goodbye to some of your friends," he said when she had piled all the articles on her bed. There still remained quite a pile of things to pack when he said: "You will want to say goodbye to some of your friends, naturally. Why don't you go and ring some of them while I finish the packing?"

Marlene looked at him helplessly. She had never in her life been so taken command of, but she did as he said, and by evening all that remained in the house was the furniture which belonged to the estate and all she had to pack was her overnight bag.

Two of her oldest friends came to the cottage to see her after Juan de Montserrat had gone. Both girls worked on the estate in various capacities. Molly was a secretary and Brenda looked after some of the animals. They arrived together full of curiosity about her new job.

"Well, I think it's a jolly good idea," Molly said

when Marlene had satisfied their curiosity. "I envy you."

"I think it's very romantic," Brenda said dreamily.

"It's nothing of the sort," Marlene retorted indignantly. "He isn't the romantic kind."

"How do you know?" demanded Brenda.

"I just do, that's all."

"Just because he didn't make a pass at you when he took you out to dinner?"

"That among other things."

"Is he married?" Brenda queried.

"Very likely. I didn't ask him."

"And about how old is he?"

"Oh, I don't know. Between thirty and forty, I suppose. What difference does it make how old he is?"

"It makes a lot of difference," Brenda retorted with a wise air. "If he's not married at that age, beware."

"I'll beware all right," Marlene answered, trying to speak lightly. "I don't intend to let myself fall in love with anybody for a long time yet—if ever again. Besides, he's not my type. He's a business tycoon."

"Well, you'll write to us, anyway, and let us know how you get on, won't you?" asked Molly. "And if you're still there next summer, maybe we'll come and see you, have a holiday there."

They talked until nearly midnight, and by that time, with the full day she had had, Marlene could scarcely keep her eyes open. As she drifted off to sleep her mind dwelt for a moment or two on her future employer. Why he had come into her life at the precise moment that he had was both a mystery and something of a miracle. But romantic? Far from it. His concern had been purely that his hotels should be made more attractive. Indeed, had there been the slightest hint in his manner that he found her attractive she would not have accepted his offer.

They departed for Spain early the next morning, Marlene's boxes, packages and suitcases taking up all of the space in the large boot of the car as well as on the rear seat. His own luggage consisted of one suitcase only. He drove at speed, speaking little, and throughout the whole journey his manner could scarcely have been more formal and polite. She could not help smiling to herself when she remembered Brenda's idea of him as a romantic. Fortunately, the weather was bright with moderate to fresh winds which kept mist and fog at bay, and as it was out of the main holiday season the roads were reasonably clear of heavy traffic. To save time and an overnight stay Juan Montserrat chose to drive all night, insisting on Marlene curling up on the back seat, transferring the luggage to the front passenger seat and on the floor.

Surprisingly, she slept, and when daylight came they were approaching the French-Spanish border. He looked so fresh, she asked him if he had had some sleep.

He shook his head. "But I'm certainly ready for some breakfast. In another half an hour we shall be in Spain. We'll have it there."

They pulled up outside a charming *restaurante* built in grey stone, and as Marlene stepped out of the car the difference in the temperature was marked. For February it was mild and sunny with a slight breeze, what would be called at home balmy.

"This is a very old but very good *restaurante*," Juan informed her as he caught her looking with interest at the overhanging balconies and the lamps set high on the walls. "And a typical example of Spanish architecture."

"It's lovely. Dignified and simple. I like it," Marlene said. "Are any of your hotels like this?"

"Unfortunately, no. Modern hotels tend to look all alike anywhere in the world, largely, I suppose, because they are not designed by the architects who live in the country, but by big combines. True, they have balconies, but the end result is that they look like hundreds of little matchboxes stuck together. But my hotels at Blanes are not *ultra*-modern. Those overlooking the bay have balconies with the traditional black railings. The one at Pineda is very modern, I'm afraid, and so is the one in Lloret."

Marlene suddenly realized that she did not know specifically how many hotels Juan de Montserrat owned. He had been rather vague about it, and she, stupidly, had not asked. She did so as they entered the restaurant.

"Six," he answered promptly. "Did I not tell you?"

"Six!" she echoed in some alarm. "But—but how on earth am I going to be able to look after all the plants and flowers in six hotels?" She was beginning to have a faint suspicion that this man had lured her here under somewhat false pretences.

"Do not worry," he told her calmly. "Whatever help you find you need you have only to tell me."

But this also sounded vague. She had no car. How was she to get from one hotel to the other to look after things adequately? She had been so eager to get away, once the idea had been put into her head, that she had not thought of all these things. She had not had time to think. Señor de Montserrat had seen to that.

Once inside, Montserrat was greeted warmly by a man Marlene took to be the proprietor from the formal way he was dressed, and for what seemed four or five minutes the two talked rapidly in Spanish, of which Marlene did not understand a word. That was another thing, she decided. She must learn the language as soon as possible, not simply 'pick it up' by degrees, or what would amount to trial and error and a great deal of embarrassment and difficulty.

Breakfast was served immediately and consisted of coffee, rolls and preserves. At first, Marlene thought longingly of bacon and eggs, but she found herself enjoying the preserves which were made from oranges and lemons locally grown and preserved—far more interesting and palatable than the marmalade one bought, or even made, at home.

While they were eating, Marlene spoke to him about the necessity of learning the language.

"Ah yes," he said. "But it is an easy language to learn. I will teach you myself, so there is no need to worry, and your English will be extremely useful to us during the holiday season. Indeed, all the year round. Many more people are taking winter holidays nowadays. It is better for us than to have the hotels empty the whole winter, even though we do not make much money."

"Yes, yes, I'm sure it is. But I want to learn the language *properly*," she protested.

He gave her a somewhat haughty stare. "And I shall teach you properly, Miss Sheridan. I have all the books necessary in my library. I can assure you, you will not find a school for English in Blanes."

"No, I—I suppose not. I'm sorry, I didn't mean to be rude."

"That is quite all right," he said loftily. "We shall be very businesslike about it, rest assured. We shall set aside a given time, say, three times a week, and you will soon learn, especially hearing it spoken by the maids and waiters, and the shopkeepers and so forth."

"You—speak excellent English yourself," she ventured. "Where did you learn?"

"It is so long ago I cannot remember," he answered

in an odd tone of voice. "And now, if you have finished your breakfast, we had better be going."

During the rest of the journey he talked exclusively about his hotels and their workings, then went on to talk about her part.

"Do you drive a car?" he asked.

"I drove the one provided by the estate," she told him.

"Good. You will need one for travelling to and from the hotels. You will have to learn to drive on the right side of the road, of course, but you will soon get used to it. Tomorrow I shall take you on a tour of the hotels. You can drive and I will be the passenger, that way you will find your way around much quicker. I have a spare car, a smaller one than this. You can have it for your own use. Keep an account of the petrol you buy, naturally. And I think you had better have a month's salary in advance."

She assured him that there was no need, as she had some money, but he would not hear of it. She was learning that he was not a man with whom to argue. He was most definitely the boss. She had been wondering whether she dared ask him if he were married, but decided against it. She would find out before long.

Driving at his usual speed and taking the main road through Perpignan, Figueras and Gerona, they arrived in Blanes in time for lunch. They approached the hotel by way of a narrow street which ran downhill and turned into the hotel at the rear. There was only just time for Marlene to catch a brief glimpse of the startingly blue sea before they came to a halt in a court-yard.

"Is this the hotel where I shall be staying?" she asked, glancing up at the four-storey building.

"Yes," he answered. "And it is also where I live."

They entered the hotel at the rear, passing the

kitchens and other domestic offices, and Juan led the way into what looked like the main office of the hotel. Seated at the desk was a dark-eyed, dark-haired girl with the most beautiful features Marlene had ever seen. At the sight of Juan the girl's eyes brightened and she rose at once, a smile on her face.

"Juan!" she exclaimed, holding out her hand to him. "You are earlier than I expected. But lunch is just about ready, I think."

Marlene noticed the use of his first name and wondered what place the girl held in his life. He shook hands with her and then turned to introduce Marlene.

"Frasquita, this is Miss Sheridan about whom I cabled to you. Miss Sheridan—Miss Quintana is my assistant and a veritable treasure."

Marlene felt herself being scrutinized by the other girl, but she smiled and held out her hand.

"How do you do, Miss Quintana."

Frasquita gave her a thin smile. "Welcome to the Hotel Marina and Blanes, Miss Sheridan. I hope you will like it here."

It sounded to Marlene that there was some doubt about it, but she thanked her and said she hoped so, too.

"Shall I show Miss Sheridan to the flat, Juan?" asked Frasquita. "I fixed it up as you said, although—"

He was fingering some letters on the desk. "No, no," he said without looking up. "I have to go up myself. I will show Miss Sheridan the flat—if you will get Manuel to take up her luggage."

"Yes, of course."

Frasquita went out, and Marlene saw that the light had gone from her eyes and her face had lost its smile. Whatever feelings Juan had or had not for her, she was in love with him.

23

CHAPTER TWO

MARLENE felt sorry for the girl. Juan was still apparently engrossed with his letters. Was he genuinely occupied or had he deliberately snubbed Frasquita? Men were often quite unaware of these things, but Marlene felt that here was something of a complex man; unpredictable, self-sufficient, hard and yet—

He glanced up suddenly and caught her looking at him. A slight smile curved his lips and he gave her a speculative look from eyes she suddenly noticed were very blue.

"Well, *señorita*, let us go, shall we? The lift is just round to the right."

They went up to the third floor which was the top. Juan opened a door into a large room with sloping ceilings at each end. The decor was most pleasing in green and gold with a leaf-green carpet, comfortable armchairs and low tables, a television set, a desk and what looked like a divan bed on one end.

"There you are," he said in a tone almost like a conjuror. "And the window looks right out on to the bay."

Marlene crossed the room in some bewilderment. Surely this room was much too well appointed for an employee? But when she reached the window and looked out she gave an audible gasp. She had never seen anything so beautiful—a wide expanse of clear blue sky, soft, undulating hills in the curve of the bay and a brilliant blue sea. Brightly coloured fishing boats were moored at the quayside, and to complete the scene, one or two yachts were dotted here and there on the water, their white sails showing up vividly against the sea and sky.

"Well?" queried Juan de Montserrat, joining her.

"It's simply unbelievable except on picture post-cards. Does it always look like this?"

"Generally, yes. But today I think the sun has shone especially for you. Most of the summer it's like this, of course, but it does rain sometimes. But even then it's beautiful—like a woman who even when sad can look enchanting."

Marlene gave him a surprised look. Perhaps Brenda was right, after all. He *could* be romantic when he chose.

"I—can see what you mean," she managed to answer. She glanced around the room again. "You can't mean that I'm to have this room?"

"Of course. Why not? Those of my staff who live in all have rooms on this floor. This room is, after all, only a bed-sitting room. Through that door," he added, pointing to the opposite end of the room, "there is a small bathroom, next door to that a minute kitchen. I have a similar flatlet right opposite to your own."

"Overlooking the bay?"

"No, no." He glanced at his watch. "Now I will leave you to tidy up for lunch. How long will you need? Five, ten minutes?"

Marlene, who never liked to keep people waiting any longer than she could help, replied that she would need no longer than five.

"Very well. I will knock on your door in five minutes' time."

As he opened the door to leave, Manuel, a youth of about seventeen, stood there carrying four of her pieces of luggage, one in each hand and one under either arm. Marlene opened her bag to give him

25

something, but guessing her intention. Juan prevented her.

"No, no. No tip. You are not a guest here, you are now a member of the staff. He will do as you ask, but do not give him money. I do that."

He spoke sharply in rapid Spanish to the boy. Manuel's big brown eyes looked large at his employer as he put down the cases.

"*Si, señor, si,*" he said in a startled voice, and disappeared before Marlene could even thank him.

"Do not tip any of the staff," Juan told her sternly. "I absolutely forbid it. Five minutes, *señorita,*" he added, glancing once more at his watch.

Marlene resisted the temptation to say : "*Si, señor.*" He might think she was laughing at him. And really, there was nothing at which to laugh, except perhaps at Brenda's idea of Juan de Montserrat being in the slightest degree a romantic figure in spite of what he had said at the window. He was a business man, an authoritarian.

She also glanced at her watch. She would have to move if she wanted to change—which she did, she decided, looking at her crumpled suit. But something made her look at her watch again. It was three-thirty —and Frasquita had said they were 'just in time for lunch'!

Marlene whipped off her suit and flung it on the bed, then picked up her overnight bag and hurried into the bathroom. She was drying her face when it occurred to her that the Spaniards took all their meals late—a siesta in the afternoon—what was left of it after a late lunch—and dinner about nine or ten o'clock in the evening. A change of living indeed for herself.

She decided to wear a coat-dress, and was just inserting a red spotted scarf at the neck when there was a knock on the door.

"One moment, please," she called out, and hastily put the finishing touches to her hair and make-up.

When she opened the door she expected to see some annoyance on his face, though she had only kept him waiting a minute or so, but his glance took in her appearance and she was gratified to see approval.

"*Bueno, señorita*. Good. I like a woman to dress well. Shall we go down?"

Marlene began to feel a slight rebellion against the way he handed out approval and disapproval, but told herself that she would have to remember that he *was* her employer for at least a few months. Rushed into it she might have been, but it had, after all, been her choice, and she must expect him to be a little high-handed at times. She must, however, get a few things straight before very long. Living in the same house as her employer could have grave disadvantages. She must have proper free time. In her working hours she would have to take certain treatment, a certain attitude from him, but in her own time—

Juan Montserrat, Frasquita and Marlene had their meal in a private room next to the office, waited on by a young woman with coal-black hair and dark eyes called Micaela.

"This room," Juan explained to Marlene, "is my sitting room and general purpose room. Apart from myself, you and Frasquita are the only other members of my staff who will use it. It is reserved for the very senior members of my staff only. And here, of course, I entertain important business men and so on."

Marlene wondered whether Frasquita would resent her coming. Until now she and Juan de Montserrat would have been accustomed to eating alone together. Frasquita spoke little during the meal—one which Marlene found quite elaborate. Five or six plates, one on top of the other, were set in each place. The Spaniards, it seemed, were not fanatics about having hot plates, as were the English. After the soup came fish, a delicious sole, freshly caught here at Blanes, she was told. Then followed chicken and rice with succulent ham. Marlene found it most curious that the vegetables were not served with the chicken but as a separate course. Cheese and biscuits were followed by fruit, and as if these were not enough, sweetmeats of Toledo marzipan were placed on the table, the whole meal accompanied by a lovely white sparkling wine like champagne. No wonder the Spaniards needed a siesta, Marlene thought. She was beginning to feel the need of one herself.

Towards the end of the meal Marlene felt she really must draw Frasquita into the conversation as Juan had addressed most of his remarks to herself.

"You speak very good English, *señorita*," she said. "Where did you learn?"

Frasquita turned her sleek head. "I was taught by the very best of teachers—Señor de Montserrat."

"Oh yes, of course."

"We have many English visitors to the hotel, also," added Frasquita.

"Have you any at present?"

But Frasquita made no reply. It was Juan who answered. "This week we have a German party. Next week—or rather for the next two weeks—we have an English party."

"And—and do you both speak German?" Marlene asked in surprise.

"Enough," answered Juan. "But the Hotel Marina is more popular with the English than any other nationality—except Spanish, of course."

He changed the subject then, and when the meal was over detained her further for a few minutes.

"There are things we have to discuss, Miss Sheridan, as I am sure you will realize. But you will need to rest for a while, even if you do not actually have our traditional siesta. Shall we say at five o'clock here?"

"Of course."

Marlene went up to her room fully intending to unpack her things, but to her surprise her clothes were all hanging in the spacious wardrobe and her other things put neatly away in the drawers. Even her books were set out on the bookshelves and the various small ornaments she had brought with her ranged out on a table. On one low table there were even some roses.

Marlene sniffed their fragrance, then frowned slightly. Who had put them here? And who had done her unpacking? In spite of what Juan de Montserrat had said to Manuel she simply could not accept services like this without saying 'thank you' at least. But suddenly, no doubt as a result of the excellent lunch as well as the travel, she felt drowsy. Why not? she asked herself. When in Rome, do as the Romans do, and when in Spain have a siesta. She threw back the cover of the divan and within minutes of her head touching the pillow she felt her senses leaving her.

Some time later she awoke to the sound of a knock on her door to find it was quite dark. She called out 'come in' and vainly tried to find the table lamp in the unfamiliar surroundings. But the light was switched on by Micaela, the young girl who had served their lunch.

"Excuse, please, *señorita*," the girl said carefully. "Señor de Montserrat say tea is ready downstairs."

Marlene glanced at her watch and gave a gasp of dismay. He had said five o'clock, and it was now nearly six.

"Tell Señor de Montserrat that I shall be down at once, please."

29

"*Si, señorita.*"

She ran a comb hurriedly through her long fair hair. She really should have done it up for the evening, but there was no time now, and certainly no time to change. What would he think of her?

When she entered the room where they had had lunch he was sitting on a settee looking through some papers. On a small table nearby stood a tray of tea.

"Señor de Montserrat, I'm so sorry. Do forgive me. I'm afraid I overslept," she said at once.

He looked up and eyed her in his scrutinizing way she was beginning to find most disconcerting. But he said easily: "That is quite all right. I guessed what had happened. Do please sit down—and perhaps you would be good enough to pour out tea."

"Thank you." She sat down and picked up the silver teapot. "Do you always have tea? I thought it was only an English custom."

"The Spaniards don't usually, but of course when we have English people staying at the hotels, then it is served, and I do sometimes have it. Today, I thought you might like it."

"That's very kind of you."

"Not at all. Tomorrow, I shall have tea-making facilities put in the kitchen in your flat. There is already a supply of crockery, some coffee and biscuits and a kettle."

Marlene wondered if they had been put there for her benefit or whether someone else had used the flat before her, but before she could perhaps ask the question he spoke again.

"There are a few matters we did not discuss in detail earlier. One of these is your salary. I propose to pay you—" He mentioned a sum almost twice her salary on the estate back home.

"But—but I can't accept as much as that!" she

felt bound to protest, and told him what her salary had been.

"Your honesty does you credit," he said, "but my mind is made up. You will have more responsibility here and you may find the work more demanding and even less interesting, though I hope not. So please, we will say no more about salary. The next thing is the question of free time. You could, of course, be an entirely free agent and have time off when it suits you and your work. Indeed, I hope you *will* feel free. But I think it best if you have certain days and week-ends free so that neither I nor anyone else will call upon you in your free time. Do you agree about that?"

"It sounds the best thing," she said in agreement.

"Well then, what about every evening free from—five or six? Er—every week-end and other days by arrangement, and of course, the *fiestas*, if you wish."

"That sounds very generous. Surely the rest of your staff work much longer hours?"

"Most of my other staff have siesta time. The waiters and waitresses have evenings and days off in their turn. It is different for them. Why must you question everything, *señorita*?" he asked sharply.

"I—I'm just trying to be fair, that's all," she protested.

"And you think that I am not?"

"Of course not. I—I simply thought that perhaps you were being over-generous with me because I'm a —foreigner, and I didn't want to take anything for granted, or unfair advantage."

He smiled then. "You English and your sense of fair play! But you must also keep in mind that as the employer of a great many people I am not accustomed to having almost everything I say questioned."

"I see."

31

Obviously he wanted her clearly to understand that they were employer and employee. Just in case she had any romantic designs on him?

"You do not 'see' at all, *señorita*, but no matter. I do not like arguments. The other matter about which I wished to speak is our mode of address. As you will have noticed, I do not doubt, Frasquita calls me Juan. This is merely for convenience and first names are only observed between my senior staff and myself and when we are alone. As the three of us will meet each other frequently at meals and so on will it be better if we all use first names. This will also prevent any misunderstandings."

He was quite astute, Marlene concluded. Evidently he wanted to scotch any misapprehension she might have been under that there was any special relationship between himself and Frasquita. Either that, or he wanted to keep it secret.

"Very well, *señor*—or rather, Juan. Mine, as I am sure you know, is Marlene."

He nodded. "In Spanish we would say Mah-lay-nay. Would you mind?"

"Not at all. In English yours would be—"

"John."

She smiled. "John—I like that. What would happen if I called you by that name?"

There was an odd expression on his face. "Please do not. I forbid it."

She was unaccustomed to being spoken to in this way. She eyed him with cold anger.

"As you're my employer, Señor de Montserrat, I will do my best to comply with your wishes, but I will not be spoken to as if I were a child. It's enough to say what you do or do not like."

He met her angry gaze with a haughty look of his own, then suddenly his features relaxed. "Then we

32

understand each other. Now. Tomorrow I will take you on a tour of my hotels. After that, it is all yours, as the English say."

His English was so perfect, it was difficult to believe that he was not an Englishman, except perhaps that he spoke a little too carefully, and had that hauteur one usually associates with wealthy Spaniards. Whether she would be happy working for him she was not sure. Perhaps it was too soon to tell.

"Is it possible for me to see the rest of the hotel here this evening?" she asked, thinking that she might as well make a start. She had nothing else to do except perhaps read. "I can find my own way around, if you're going to be busy."

"I do have things to attend to, yes. Dinner, by the way, is at nine-thirty—late by your standards, I suppose. But our night life does not start until about eleven o'clock."

"And at what time do you start the day?"

"It varies. In the days before tourism, ten o'clock, maybe. Now, those concerned with the tourist trade have to be up early. In the country, perhaps, they can stick to the old ways."

"Odd. In England it's the country people who go to bed early and get up early."

He rose, indicating that the interview was over. "I make no stipulation about what time your day starts, anyhow. It will be for you to decide whether you adopt our way of life or adhere to your own."

"I expect I shall adopt a modified version of yours," answered Marlene. "But do we not all have breakfast together?"

He shook his head. "No. Frasquita lives with her parents and has breakfast before she arrives, and I have been accustomed to having mine in my room. Perhaps you would like to do the same. You can, if

33

you wish, have it in here, of course. Micaela will bring it to you."

But Marlene would not hear of that. "I'm sure Micaela has enough to do. I shall have it in my room and prepare it myself. I have only a light breakfast, usually."

"As you wish. Get anything you require from the kitchen." He opened the door and indicated that she should precede him.

The foyer was full of people, and as soon as Juan emerged he was approached by someone. Of Frasquita there was no sign. Marlene moved on and decided to take a look at the patio he had told her about.

She was pleasantly surprised and thought it had distinct possibilities. There were swinging hammocks, raffia chairs and small tables and the whole area was surrounded by high walls. These showed evidence of climbing plants and here and there were containers which had held other kinds. There was very little in bloom at present, which she thought a pity, as the temperature was mild compared with that she had left behind. Chilly, perhaps, but not terribly cold. In some of the tubs dotted about there had evidently been roses, but they looked a very sorry lot now. In mild winters at home one could often gather rosebuds on Christmas Day. Surely they could be persuaded to bloom here in weather like this? Geraniums, too, would go on until frosts killed them.

She glanced at the walls again. Panels of trellis would be good there, the white plastic kind which always looked clean and did not look scruffy when a fresh coat of paint was required as in the case of the old wooden ones. And the tubs were a very uninteresting-looking lot. Would Juan sanction the spending of money? She was surprised that he had not ordered some better ones himself. But perhaps he had been

34

too busy. Her mind began to plan, her imagination to work on colour schemes, to make a paved garden which as well as being colourful would be harmonious. She should have brought a notebook with her. She had brought some gardening books with her, and could plan this garden this very evening. She would go upstairs and get a notebook. She would make a sketch of the place as it was and how she would like to see it, then she would sketch it in the coloured crayons she and her father always used when planning a new scheme.

She was going through the door when she almost collided with someone. She murmured an apology and was about to pass on when she was halted by a voice saying in very good English :

"Don't run away, Miss Sheridan."

Marlene looked at the man in surprise. "You know my name?"

He smiled. He was an extremely good-looking young man—of about her own age, Marlene guessed—and he reminded her of someone.

"Allow me to introduce myself. My name is Ramon —Ramon Quintana."

"Quintana? Then you must be—"

"Frasquita's brother. So you see we are almost acquainted already."

"Oh. Oh yes, of course. Very nice." He was barring the way, and teeming with ideas as her brain was. Marlene was more anxious to have her notebook and pencils so that she could get to work. "If you will excuse me, *señor*—"

"Not until you promise to have a drink with me. Then—"

He broke off as Frasquita appeared. "Ah, so there you are, Ramon," she said in a cordial voice. "I was looking for you—to introduce you to Marlene."

35

He smiled. "I have just introduced myself and was asking—er—Miss Sheridan to have a drink with me."

Marlene was beginning to feel rather cornered. If she went upstairs now to get her things it would look rude, and she did not want to start her life in a foreign country by upsetting people. But before she could say anything at all, Frasquita spoke again.

"I wonder, Ramon, if you would show Marlene over the rest of the hotel? Juan thought—"

"A pleasure," Ramon cut in brightly. "But first a drink. I insist."

Marlene suppressed a sigh. The pair of them were very persistent. She would have to accept Ramon's invitation if she were going to get anything done tonight. And if Juan had suggested it—

"All right—thank you very much. But I—"

She broke off as she found herself being propelled towards the cocktail bar. The Spaniards were all masterful, it seemed.

There were few people in the bar. Marlene caught a glimpse of a crowded restaurant which meant that most of the guests were at dinner.

"What will you have, *señorita*?" Ramon enquired, choosing a comfortable corner.

"Er—sherry?"

"Ah! *Jerez*!"

He pronounced it so oddly, to her ears, she couldn't have begun to say it. And Juan had said Spanish was an easy language to learn! Ramon laughed at the puzzled expression on her face.

"I must teach you how to speak Spanish, *señorita*," he said, beckoning a waiter.

She laughed with him somewhat ruefully. "I believe Señor de Montserrat is going to teach me."

"Ah—Juan," he repeated. "Of course." Marlene noticed that the smile had gone from his face. But before she could ask him what he meant or what he was thinking, he went on : "Well, I suppose he will be very severe and teach you all the grammar and so on like a schoolmaster. I can teach you to speak it the easy way. Now take the word *jerez*——sherry. It is easy if you remember that the letter *j* is aspirated, and that *z* is pronounced *th*. *Jerez*—so. Now you try it."

She tried, but it did not sound in the least as he had said it. They both laughed, and as Marlene happened to glance across the room she saw Juan looking at them.

"Now try it again," Ramon said. "And this time, remember that the letter *e* is pronounced *ay*."

She did so, and it sounded better, but she did not see how it was going to be a very easy language to learn. *Jerez* had only five letters, and each one of them had a pronunciation far different from her own language. Even the *r* was trilled more. She voiced the thought.

"Don't worry," laughed Ramon. "There are others much easier. *Jerez* is quite a difficult one really. *El tren*, for instance—the train. Only the spelling is different. It sounds the same and it means the same."

"Well, thank goodness something does," she said, laughing.

The waiter brought their drinks. A dark, full-bodied sherry for her which tasted wonderful, and a dark, Spanish brandy for Ramon.

"Where did you learn to speak English?" Marlene asked him. "You speak it very well."

"I learned in various ways. A little at school, then I had an English friend, and Spain has become very popular with the English."

"Do you meet many English in the course of your work?" she asked somewhat absentmindedly, as she could see Juan from time to time, and felt she should

37

be about her own work.

Ramon laughed. "You English! You are always talking about work. Let us talk about some other things. Tell me about yourself. What do you like to do to amuse yourself?"

But Marlene felt she had talked enough. "If you will excuse me, Ramon, I must go to my room to get a notebook and some pencils—which is where I was on my way to when you first saw me."

He rose with her. "Ah yes, the tour of the hotel. I will wait for you here."

But she wanted to go back to the patio garden alone and get some ideas down while they were still fresh in her mind.

"There is something I must do first," she told him firmly. "I'll meet you here in about half an hour— unless, of course, you would rather not wait."

"To wait for you will be a pleasure, Señorita Marlene," he said gallantly.

Half amused and half bemused by his Spanish courtesy, Marlene left him and made her way to the lift. She noticed one or two people wearing evening clothes, and suddenly became aware that she was still wearing her coat-dress. She really ought to slip into something a little more suitable, she thought.

A quick look in her wardrobe found a long black skirt. That would fill the bill perfectly, she decided. It took only minutes to slip into it and top it with a white blouse. Her notebook, drawing block and coloured pencils she put in a folder and went downstairs again.

There was still no one outside. Marlene sat at one of the tables and made a rough sketch of the area, working quickly as ideas began to flow into her head.

First, the walls. Bougainvillaea. That surely would do well out of doors in this climate and in such a

38

sheltered garden. Clematis, too, of course—and to provide a restful corner, the cool *plumbago capensis*. And a fountain. Couldn't there be a cool fountain with goldfish and even waterlilies?

Her crayons flew across her drawing paper. Juan had said this job might not be so interesting. It was wonderful. Plenty of scope. She suddenly became aware of someone looking over her shoulder. Marlene swung around, hoping it would be Juan coming to see what she was doing, but it was Ramon.

"Very nice. Very nice indeed. It will look beautiful. You are very clever, and you have also artistic talent. I hope Montserrat appreciates you."

There was something in the way he said the latter part of his words that caused her to look up sharply. Then, her eyes down on her work again, she answered:

"If he appreciates my work and allows me to carry out my ideas that will be enough."

He pulled up a chair and sat down at the table with her. "Why did you come back with him?"

"I wanted to—to get away—for a change."

"Ah! Then you did not come because you were—shall I say—attracted to Montserrat?"

Marlene glanced up swiftly. "Certainly not, Señor Quintana!" she told him indignantly. "How dare you even think such a thing?"

"I humbly beg your pardon, *señorita*. But I am glad to hear it all the same."

His glance went to the door and an ironical smile curved his lips. Marlene swung around, but there was no one there.

"Was there someone—"

"Only Montserrat. He vanished when he saw you were not alone."

Marlene stared at him and threw a worried look in the direction of the door.

"You—don't suppose he heard—"

Ramon shrugged. "Hard to say. But if he did perhaps it was a good thing."

Marlene drew an exasperated breath. "I do wish you'd stop this kind of talk once and for all, *señor*. Señor de Montserrat saw my work, liked it and hired me. I accepted because my father had—had just—died and I wanted a change of scene. And that's all."

Ramon smiled unabashed. "I believe you—but who can read the mind of Juan de Montserrat? He is—what you say—a cold fish, but he is a man, and you are a very attractive woman."

Marlene rose to her feet and collected her papers together. "I'm sorry, but if you're going to persist in this line of talk I must leave you."

"O.K., O.K., I will stop, I promise. You can't leave me now after I've waited for you for nearly an hour—and you *did* say you would be back in about *half* an hour."

"An hour!" Marlene glanced at her watch. It was true. It was now well over an hour since she went upstairs. A punctual sort of person who never liked to keep anyone waiting, she felt bound to apologize.

"Perhaps you wouldn't mind showing me the rest of the hotel, now?" she added.

"Delighted."

As they went along Marlene made notes. The plants in the foyer and lounge left much to be desired and so did those in the dining room. Marlene began to feel quite dismayed. To have everything as she herself would like to see it would cost quite a great deal of money. She would have to work it out, do some seed-sowing and propagating. Juan had said something about having a greenhouse somewhere. She must speak to him about it. The balconies of the bedrooms, especially those at the front of the hotel, could, of course, look good with geraniums. There was evidence that some had been growing there, but they looked a poor lot at present. Perhaps she could fill in with some annual trailers for this year.

"Well, I think you have seen everywhere," Ramon said at last. "So now I suggest we go downstairs and have another drink."

Marlene frowned a little. She was not all that fond of drinking. Besides—

"I really do think I ought to get a few ideas down while they're still fresh in—"

He shook his head. "There is one word you must learn. It is a very good one and you will hear it a lot in Spain."

"What's that?"

"*Mañana*. It means tomorrow. The work will still be there tomorrow, your ideas will come back. You have done enough work for one day. Take your books to your room. And this time I shall come with you and wait outside your door—unless you are kind enough to ask me in. I understand you have Montserrat's flat."

Marlene drew in a swift breath. "Oh, no—"

Ramon laughed shortly. "Didn't you know?"

She shook her head. "I—I thought it was odd—such a well appointed flat for a mere employee."

Ramon pressed the lift button to take them to the top floor, but said nothing. Recalling his other remarks, Marlene could well hazard a guess as to what was going through his mind.

"It was very kind of him," she said stiffly, "but I shall ask to be moved."

Ramon's brows arched. "I should like to be there—invisibly, of course—when you do."

She knew what he meant, and quailed at the idea herself. What would she say to him? What reason

41

could she give, except perhaps to say that she did not feel comfortable at the thought that he had given up his flat for her? Why had he done so? Surely he had realized that it might give a wrong impression?

As they stepped out of the lift Juan himself was waiting to go down. He looked from one to the other, faint disapproval showing in his expression. He stepped into the lift, however, without a word. Marlene frowned worriedly. Did he think she was taking Ramon into the flat. By modern British standards there was no harm, nor would there be by Marlene's own standards, but was it the sort of thing which was frowned upon in Spain? She had no intention of inviting him in, in any case. She unlocked the door, dropped her folder on the nearest chair and was out again in two seconds.

Ramon gave her an amused smile. "Afraid of me— or of Montserrat?"

"I'm not afraid of either of you," she told him. "First, there is no point in our going into the flat. You've asked me to have a drink and it will soon be time for dinner. And second, I feel I should find out what Señor de Montserrat's rule is before entertaining in my quarters."

"I should have thought you were free to do as you please in your own time."

Marlene agreed with him, but did not say so. She was beginning to think that, when she started to find her way around Blanes, it might be better if she were to find a flat somewhere else. Being under the eye of one's employer so closely could have distinct disadvantages.

When they went downstairs again there was no sign of Juan. About half an hour before dinner Frasquita joined them and invited Ramon to stay to dinner.

"It is allowed," she explained to Marlene. "Juan

42

and I often have friends to dine—and of course Ramon, as my brother, is a frequent guest." She glanced at her watch. "We shall also be expected to join Juan in a quarter of an hour's time for cocktails."

"A royal command," Ramon said sarcastically.

Frasquita shot him a barbed look. "It is a matter of courtesy."

It was evident that Ramon, at least, did not care very much for Juan, and Marlene wondered why.

CHAPTER THREE

DINNER was a most uncomfortable affair. Juan spoke little, Ramon talked too much and Frasquita was very much on edge. What was it between the three of them? For herself, she could do no more than respond to Ramon's conversation. She tried to talk to Juan.

"I've made some sketches of the patio-garden," she began.

But he cut her short. "I don't like to talk about work at meal times, Marlene. We will discuss it all tomorrow."

"*Mañana*," said Ramon. "I told you, didn't I?"

Marlene laughed briefly. "Ramon has been teaching me a little Spanish."

"Really?" Juan said coolly. "And did he tell you that *mañana*, as well as meaning tomorrow, can also mean in the morning?"

"Well no, he didn't."

"*Si, señorita. Para levantarse temprano, es necesario estudiar aprender una lengud*," he said in rapid Spanish.

Ramon answered him in Spanish, but Juan held up his hand.

"Enough. We will speak English until Marlene learns a little Spanish, then we will use both until she becomes fluent."

By the time they had eaten Marlene began to feel incredibly tired, especially as Juan had put on a gramophone record of guitar music. She leaned back in her chair, closed her eyes to rest them for a moment and found her senses slipping away from her. She opened her eyes with a start.

"I would suggest an early night for you," Juan said. "We had a long journey, and you couldn't have slept very soundly in the back of the car."

"Thank you, I think I will, if you'll excuse me," she answered, rising to her feet.

At this Ramon rose too. "Will you excuse me, also? I have another engagement."

He went out at the same time as Marlene and accompanied her to the lift.

He smiled and touched her cheek. "Well, *señorita, hasta la vista.*"

"What does that mean?"

"Until we meet again. It will not be long, I hope. Tomorrow evening, perhaps? Tonight you are tired, but tomorrow at this time the evening will be only just beginning."

Marlene looked at her watch and saw that it was already eleven o'clock. These Spaniards certainly kept late hours.

But she shook her head at Ramon's invitation. "I'm sorry, but I really do feel I should get my bearings before I make any plans of my own."

He shook his head admonishingly. "Maybe I'll see you, anyway. I often come in here."

They said goodnight, and Ramon started to walk away when Marlene suddenly thought of something.

"Ramon—"

"Yes?" he asked, turning back.

"What was it Juan said in Spanish?"

He laughed. "Oh, it was nothing important. He was just scoring off me, that's all. He said : It is necessary to study in order to learn a language. He hates it if he thinks somebody is treading on what he imagines is his preserves. But who cares? He can teach you

45

grammar, as he undoubtedly will, and I will teach you as many sayings and phrases as I can. It's easier that way. So *hasta la vista* once again, sweet *señorita*."

"*Hasta la vista*," she answered almost absent-mindedly, and smiled to herself as she went up in the lift. Ramon was right. But why was there this tension, this dislike between the two men? Perhaps it was merely one of differences in personality. They rubbed each other the wrong way. All the same, she was glad that Ramon did not work here. She would have hated such an unpleasant atmosphere.

She set her alarm and was asleep almost as soon as her head touched her pillow. The following morning she realized she had forgotten to go to the kitchen last night to get something for breakfast. She went into the small kitchen, but the cupboard, like that of Old Mother Hubbard of the nursery rhyme, was bare. She was wondering what to do when there came a knock at the door and Micaela entered with a breakfast tray.

"Oh, Micaela, you shouldn't have. But how kind of you."

"The Señor, he say—to bring—"

'The Señor', it seemed, always had his own way. "Well, thank you, Micaela. I'll bring the tray down to the kitchen, don't you bother about it."

There was tea, rolls and butter and some of the same kind of delicious lemon preserve they had on their journey. Marlene made a mental note to stock up her little kitchen with a few necessities and not to forget, in future, to bring up milk and rolls at night from the main kitchen.

For the itinerary of the other hotels Marlene wore a trouser suit in bottle green set off with a yellow sweater. Juan was in the office when she went downstairs. She felt herself well scrutinized when she

46

entered, but he made no comment on her appearance.

"Those sketches you made of the patio-garden," he said. "Did you bring them down?"

"Well, no, I didn't. I think perhaps I'd like to work on them a little more before you see them," she said on the spur of the moment, suddenly realizing that she should have brought her folio to take some notes as they went around. "But I'll go and get them if you'd like to see them."

"Yes, I would. Get them, if you don't mind, and I'll wait for you outside in the car."

Marlene could have kicked herself. So far, she was not making a very good impression on her new employer. Yesterday evening she had overslept and he had had to send someone to waken her. This morning he had somehow found out that she had forgotten to call in at the kitchen for something for breakfast so had had to send up a tray. And now she had forgotten to bring down her portfolio. Added to which, she had a strong feeling that he had disapproved of her being with Ramon yesterday evening. The latter could only be that he disliked Ramon himself. Ought she to respect his feelings in this or show him that in her own time she intended to do what she wanted to do and see whom she wanted to see? She was not sure. Normally, she liked to please people, but if Juan de Montserrat was going to be dictatorial—she must allow him a certain amount of authority over her, naturally, but—

As she snatched up her portfolio and hurried downstairs again she wondered how women were regarded in Spanish society. She had a vague idea that they were not so emancipated as those in England or America and some other European countries, and though they might not be exactly subservient they were, in a way, controlled or defended—protected and certainly restrained.

But she was not Spanish, she thought with sudden defiance, and though she would do her best to carry out this man's wishes as her employer, she was certainly going to retain her freedom.

"I'm sorry to keep you waiting," she said as she joined him. "I meant to have brought all this down with me without having to go back up for it because I want to make notes as I go along this morning."

"Perhaps you had your mind on other things. The dashing Ramon, for instance."

As he spoke he started the car and turned into the road which ran parallel with the sea. For a moment or two Marlene's attention was caught by the beauty of it all : the high, wide expanse of sky, the incredibly blue sea even at this time of year. But she felt she really could not let his remark about Ramon pass.

"I would like to get one thing clear, Señor de Montserrat. If, as you told me, my evenings will be free, I considered myself free yesterday evening, and I would like it to be clearly understood that what I do in my free time is entirely my own affair."

There was a silence which could virtually be felt. For a moment Marlene feared she had gone too far, but she felt she simply had to make a stand.

"Then let me, also, make one thing clear," he said in a staccato voice. "When the things you do in your free time affect your efficiency, then it *is* my affair."

For a moment her anger threatened to boil over and a dozen angry retorts hovered on her lips, but she forced herself to simmer down. Of what use would it be to prolong the argument, to tell him that her forgetting her papers this morning was nothing whatever to do with Ramon? She had not even given him a thought. On balance, Juan had been very generous and extremely thoughtful. He was paying her a good salary and was entitled to good service as well as a certain amount of deference. She had made her point. She would let it rest there.

"By the way, Juan," she said after a minute or two, "I'd like to thank you for sending up my breakfast this morning. I forgot to call in at the kitchen last night. But it won't happen again. I'm not usually so forgetful."

He inclined his head. "Please do not worry about it. It takes time to settle down in a new country and a new job."

His kinder, gentler tone gave her an intense feeling of pleasure. She smiled, her spirits rising.

"I'm so looking forward to seeing your other hotels," she told him. "I made a lot of sketches last night— though I'm afraid you might find some of my ideas rather costly."

"Changes for the better almost invariably cost money," he answered. "I'm prepared to spend a little. I thought we would go first to Pineda, which is south from Blanes, then back to Blanes for lunch, and to Lloret this afternoon."

"What—no siesta?" she asked, smiling.

"A short one, if you wish. Indeed, it might be advisable. Our lunches tend to be a little large. But I have never somehow acquired the long siesta."

"I'm sure I shan't, either. *Is* the *siesta* still practised?" she queried. "Or is it just the older people who sleep?" From what he had just said she thought it must be so.

"Well, it's not as widespread as it used to be, but you will certainly find the shops closed throughout the afternoon, but then, of course, they are open until late at night. And in country districts it is still adhered to. It is natural, really. Generally, the afternoons are too hot for work. The evenings are much cooler."

"Are your parents hoteliers?" she asked, wondering why he had not acquired the siesta habit.

"No," he answered abruptly. "They are not."

There was such an edge to his voice she fell silent. Maybe he did not like personal questions. But before long they arrived at Pineda.

"We will go first to the Hotel Bella Vista. Not a very original name, alas, but attractive enough to the average holidaymaker."

Marlene found she was more interested in the village than in the prospect of seeing the hotel as they drove up narrow streets flanked by low villas one would call bungalows at home.

"In the summer these houses will be spilling over with flowers," Juan told her. "And that is how I would like my hotels to look."

"It shouldn't be difficult," Marlene answered, "especially in a climate like this. I expect watering is the main problem, but I have an idea about that."

"Oh? What is it?"

"Covering the soil in the tubs and pots with black plastic to conserve the moisture."

"Very good! And plastic is cheap enough anyhow."

They drove along the side of a most attractive-looking square with a central fountain and seats beneath some trees which had hanging branches rather like that of the weeping willow.

"What are they called?" she asked curiously.

"It is the melias. In the summer they bear a most attractive bluish-purple flower. In fact the square is called Melias."

Marlene was beginning to look forward to the summer. It would be interesting to discover how much earlier everything bloomed here.

The Hotel Bella Vista was a five-storey modern hotel. Marlene looked up at the concrete-like construction with distaste.

"You won't expect flowers to cascade from all those balconies, will you?" she asked him.

He shook his head. "Good heavens, no. Here, the important places are the front of the hotel, the foyer and other public rooms. The hotel frontage being perhaps the most important, as our guests sit out here. There is nothing at the rear. A swimming pool is not necessary as the hotel is so close to the beach."

The paved area in front of the hotel was quite large with swinging hammocks, tables and chairs. Here and there squares of soil had been left in the paving for plants, but the ones there at the moment looked a sorry lot. Marlene asked why it was when, actually, the weather was not terribly cold yet.

Juan gave a philosophical lift of his shoulders. "Ramon was right to teach you the word *mañana*. You will hear it frequently. You cannot hurry a Spaniard. It is his nature. There is nothing—or at any rate few things—which cannot be done equally well tomorrow as today. He does not rush and tear around frantically trying to get this, that, and the other done today when tomorrow will do. This can be frustrating to a foreigner, but it makes the Spaniard a happy, easy-going person, pleasant to be with. Ramon is fairly typical. These plants, for instance. The man who looks after them knows that soon the weather will become cold and wet. Already, it is too cold for guests to sit out unless the sun is actually shining and there is no wind blowing from the mountains. So, he thinks why bother? In the summer, of course, it is too hot for rushing about, as you will discover, and so the natives of Spain have learned to go at a slower pace. It is in their blood."

"I see," Marlene said thoughtfully. "And do you have the *mañana* philosophy?"

For a split second he seemed to freeze and she feared she had offended him again. But he answered, "It is more pronounced in some than others, naturally. In any case, you will not find me rushing about—and I do not expect you to do so, either. What I do know is that you *care* about plants. That was evident in the way you were looking after them when I first met you."

She laughed briefly. "I certainly don't have the *mañana* complex—yet, and I'm sure I can find some plants which will give colour or look pleasing all the year round. For this reason I think tubs are better than permanent areas of soil. One can then replace plants which have passed their best with something else."

Other ideas were running through her mind, too, but she thought she had better say no more for the present. She made one or two notes, then they went back through the square of the melias trees to the other hotel.

"Now this is one of my favourites," Juan said as they drew up outside a hotel surrounded by an ever-green hedge. "It is called the Hotel del Jardin—the garden hotel. And soon you will see why."

They passed through a gateway and Marlene was agreeably surprised to find a large and attractively laid out garden in front of a hotel much smaller than the one they had just visited. There were ample lawns with trees dotted here and there, and island flower bed or two, and at the far end a swimming pool surrounded by paving or sitting out areas and here and there small spreading trees to provide shade. The whole aspect was pleasing.

"Now this looks like the work of a professional," she said with a sigh of satisfaction.

"You like it?"

"Very much. I don't really think I would change a thing."

"This is where I thought you might have your small glasshouse if you think it will be useful," Juan told her.

"It would be. The initial outlay would be an expense, of course, but in the long term it would save money. I find it much more satisfactory to grow my own plants rather than buy them from a nursery—and naturally it is cheaper."

"We will go into the finances of it later," he said. "Within reason it is not cost that counts in this particular project. We will see the inside of the hotel, then have coffee or whatever other refreshment you care for. The waiters here make very good tea."

"Coffee will be fine. It's traditional at this time in England."

"Perhaps you would like to have it out here in the garden."

The interior of the hotel was attractive enough, the lounge spacious and comfortable and the whole atmosphere one of order and efficiency. There were a fair number of guests, but not, Juan said, as many as they normally had in the summer months.

"Still, it is better than being closed altogether. We simply close the top storey."

"Do any of the staff live in?" Marlene asked.

"A few, but I like to get my staff from the village whenever possible."

They sat in a sheltered spot in the full sun and Marlene found it very pleasant indeed. She would find the work interesting enough, she thought, and she had no doubt that she would enjoy life in the sun, but she had a feeling she was going to miss the green countryside of home and having a garden of her own. She spoke some of her thoughts aloud.

"It's a pity the hotel at Blanes hasn't a garden like this."

"You can come here whenever you wish," he told her. "In any case your greenhouse will be here."

"Yes, but—"

He gave her a penetrating look. "But you are going to miss the green fields of your country."

She smiled ruefully. "I suppose so, but perhaps in time I shall fall in love with the sea."

"That may not be all you will fall in love with, *señorita*," he said surprisingly.

"What on earth do you mean by that, *señor*?"

"I mean that you might well fall in love with the Spanish people."

She was relieved that he spoke in the plural. For a moment she thought he had been referring to Ramon. To fall in love again, either with a Spaniard or anyone else was the last thing she wanted to do, but she couldn't help wondering about Juan. Why had he never married? He was rich enough and attractive enough. She would have thought a man would get tired of living in a hotel.

"I'm sure I shall like the Spanish people enough to want to stay for a while, anyway," she told him.

While they were drinking their coffee the gardener put in an appearance and Juan called him over and introduced him to Marlene. His name was Alfonso Massana and his smile added deep grooves in an already wrinkled face, weatherbeaten by the wind and sun of many years. Marlene felt she would be quite incapable of giving any orders whatever to this dignified man.

"Your garden is beautiful, Señor Massana," she told him.

He answered in Spanish and Juan interpreted. "He welcomes you to Spain, you are to call him Alfonso and he has never before met a lady gardener."

Marlene laughed. "I don't suppose he has. Professional women gardeners are not all that common in England, though I suspect that in nine homes out of ten most of the gardening is done by the wife."

"Because they have more time?"

"Heavens, no. Because they're more industrious and because they like to see the garden looking bright with flowers or find that home-grown vegetables are both nicer and cheaper."

Juan interpreted some of this conversation, too, then with a 'gracias, Alfonso', the man went on his way.

"I certainly like Alfonso," Marlene said. "But do you think he'll mind working with a woman? One thing I do know—I shan't interfere very much, if at all, with his work in the garden."

"He'll be interested to see what you do in your greenhouse, at all events," said Juan.

From Pineda they went back to Blanes to see the other hotel, a more modern one than the other and situated right on the beach. Marlene did not like it so much, though it was very well appointed. It did have a paved area, however, which would need a supply of plants and flowers, and there was no doubt about it: Marlene was going to be kept very busy. After lunch, which they had back at the Hotel Marina, and following a brief siesta time, Juan drove in the opposite direction from Pineda. This time to Lloret, a fashionable holiday resort which had numerous hotels and a busy night life.

"You can see the flamenco danced there if you wish," Juan told her. "They have top class artists and really do perform the authentic flamenco."

"Yes, I'd like that," Marlene answered, wondering whether he was actually inviting her to go with him.

55

"I expect you've seen it many times."

"It is very exciting. One cannot help but be enthralled with it."

Enthralled. Marlene had not heard that word for a very long time. He did not make a definite invitation, however, and Marlene found she was disappointed. It was foolish of her, of course. He was her employer. Why should he take her anywhere unless it was in line with her job?

Still in Blanes they passed a huge statue of a man in long robes, looking out to sea, his arms outstretched.

"That is Joaquim Ruyra," Juan told her. "He is the patron saint of the fishermen. The outstretched arms denote his blessing for a good catch. He is very much revered by the fishermen of Blanes."

Marlene found her heart warming towards these people and already was beginning to feel at one with them. She could well understand Juan's quiet pride as he spoke of 'my people' and 'my country'.

It did not take them long to reach Lloret, and apart from the sea-front, which was very lovely and picturesque, Marlene did not like it very much. Juan pointed out a particular night club where the flamenco was performed.

"I will take you there one evening," he said. "You will enjoy the show, I am sure of it."

"Oh. Oh, thank you," she said, somewhat taken aback by his invitation. "I shall look forward to it."

Juan's hotel was high on a hill among a great many others. As it was so far away from the beach it had a swimming pool as did most of the hotels. It was around here where her work would be needed most, and in the hotel foyer and other rooms. Here were no wrought iron balconies where one could grow trailing plants. It would take an army of workers and a great deal of money to decorate all these stone 'sea-view' balconies. She wondered that Juan could bear to be the owner of one of these monstrosities.

"Well, what do you think of this one?" he asked her.

She felt she simply had to be honest. "I think it's awful! There ought to be a law against anyone even designing such monstrosities, still less building them."

"And against owning one?" he queried, giving her a sidelong glance.

"What can I say to that when you own one?" she countered. "I certainly wouldn't like to be the owner of one of them myself."

"Not even if you could make a great deal of money by doing so?"

She thought for a moment, then said decisively: "No, not even then. They're a blot on the landscape."

"I agree, but they exist. You cannot escape the fact. If I may say so, you are being very unrealistic."

"Perhaps so. But I wouldn't have one on principle."

"Other people would buy them—as indeed they have, obviously, so your sticking to a principle would not change anything," he pointed out.

"I suppose not. But if, in the beginning, a sufficient number of people had refused to buy them, then the architects would have had to design something better. Not enough people care enough."

"That's true," he conceded, "but it is a *fait accompli* now, isn't it?"

"Unfortunately, yes. But I still wouldn't care to own one. Not that I would criticize anyone else—you, for instance—for being the owner of one of them."

"Thank you," he said with more than a hint of sarcasm. "I trust you have no objection to working in one?"

"How can I?"

"It is up to you. Or do your principles not go quite

so far as that?"

"I have another principle," she told him, feeling this conversation had gone far enough. "I undertook to work for you and I am both duty bound and honour bound to do my job. That goes without saying. But I must admit I shall enjoy most working in the Hotel Marina and the garden hotel at Pineda. Not that I shall neglect the others, of course," she hastened to add.

"I'm glad to hear you say so," he said with a combination of humour and sarcasm. "Er—there is one thing," he added, as she made a few notes. "By beautifying these ugly, modern hotels you will be doing a good job. It is a thought. Instead of looking at the buildings people will be looking at your flowers and so on."

Marlene thought that nothing could beautify these mountains of concrete, but she said no more on the subject. These kind of hotels were going up in every city in the world with no regard to the design particular to the individual country. This meant that every city would look the same.

Then Juan said: "One day you must go to Barcelona and visit the Spanish Village of Montjuich. It was built during the International Exhibition of Barcelona in 1929 and contains examples of all the different kinds of architecture of Spain. There is a square, town hall, houses, streets, shops and even small workshops where you can see various craftsmen at work—leather, glass, lacquered metal, lace-work—"

"Sounds interesting," Marlene said, genuinely intrigued. "That is something I shall look forward to."

She noticed that this time he did not offer to take her. But why should he? Apparently there was a good train service to Barcelona. She would simply have to go exploring on her own. A night-club was different. No doubt Juan de Montserrat had this fact in mind. A woman could hardly go into a night club alone.

"All right, then," he said decisively. "Let us leave this obnoxious hotel and go back to Blanes and have tea. Then you can show me your sketches and we will discuss your ideas."

When they arrived back in Blanes a small car stood in the courtyard. It looked new.

"Ah!" Juan exclaimed. "I was hoping this would be delivered today. Do you like it?"

Marlene looked at him uncertainly. "You—you don't mean—"

"Yes, I do mean. It's for you, to get around in." He looked at her face. "What's the matter? Don't you like the colour or something?"

It was pale green, and she liked it very much. "You didn't have to get a new car just for me. I could just as well have travelled around by train."

"You could do no such thing. It would be a sheer waste of time. Besides, there are bound to be plants and things you want to move from one place to another."

"But such an unnecessary expense. I could at least have managed with a second-hand one."

"And have it breaking down miles away from the nearest garage? Really, you are the most argumentative woman I've ever come across. Do you like the car or don't you?"

"I—I'm sorry, Juan. Yes, of course I like it. It's very good of you to get it for me. And you're quite right—it *will* save time and be extremely useful. It's simply that I wanted to spare you expense."

He regarded her with a faint smile. "That's kind of you, but I do not wish to be spared expense in this matter. I am not exactly poor. Now, we shall go inside and have tea, then talk more business. After that, if you are not too exhausted, we will begin your Spanish lessons."

He was certainly keeping her busy. She could see that there was going to be no danger of her becoming bored in this job. Or having time to think of the past —which was exactly what she wanted.

Frasquita did not appear for tea, and so Marlene and Juan were alone together.

"Is Frasquita off duty today?" she asked him.

"She is normally off every afternoon," he told her. "Actually, office hours are from nine to about two-thirty, then from five to seven-thirty. These hours have to be flexible in hotel work, naturally, but in any case she does not care for tea."

Marlene found it difficult to remember these strange ways and customs of the Spanish people. Even taking into consideration the differences in the climate of her own country she could hardly see her countrymen and women sitting in their offices until seven-thirty every evening.

"Doesn't anyone in Spain work in the afternoon?" she asked.

"Not if they can help it. But do not get the impression that the Spanish people are lazy. The siesta is a reasonable enough custom in a hot climate like ours, and in fact the Spaniard works very hard at his job. He has to. But he is not interested in a lot of hectic activity for its own sake, nor is he interested in 'getting rich quick'. For instance, you will find that Alfonso will do his work conscientiously, but he will be missing from the hours of, say, two-thirty and four-thirty."

"I expect I shall be looking for a cool spot myself," said Marlene.

Juan nodded. "I only suggested your own hours of work because I thought they would suit you better— and to make sure you *did* have some time off. You just work any kind of hours you wish. And now, where are those plans of yours?"

To Marlene's great satisfaction and relief he approved most of her ideas, especially those for the patio-garden in the Blanes hotel where they both lived.

"A small fountain would be a splendid idea," he said. "Also in front of the Hotel Bella Vista. As to growing our own plants from seed, that is entirely up to you. I know you will find it more interesting than choosing plants already grown, but you must not over-do it. Above all, do not do so for reasons of economy. Having said that, I should think the first thing to do is to site your greenhouse and get that into being. Tomorrow I will take you see the Botanical Gardens. There is also a restaurant up there in the hills. We will have lunch there."

It was not so much an invitation as an order, but obviously he considered a visit to the Gardens was in line with her job.

"And now," he went on, "how do you feel about learning a little Spanish?"

"Why, yes, certainly."

Marlene was keen, if a little breathless. They had already had quite a full day, and truth to tell she would have preferred, at this moment, to have a little time to herself to think about her plans for the gardens and hotel foyers and other rooms. But he reached in a bookcase for some books and handed her one by a Spaniard called Diaz de la Cortina.

"It is a good method," Juan told her. "And here, too, is an exercise book. This one is a dictionary. From this you will be able to compile your own list of nouns and phrases applicable to horticulture. But first, a few essential differences in the pronunciation of English and the pronunciation of Spanish."

The main differences was in the pronunciation of

61

the letters *c*, *j*, and *z*, and also *e*. *J* was aspirated like *h*. *H* was not sounded at all. In most instances *c* and *z* sounded as if one had a lisp, while *e* sounded like *a*. This she had noticed in the pronunciation of *Pineda*. As to Blanes, it sounded like Blarness. It was all quite fascinating. After pointing out these differences Juan went all around the room naming the different objects in Spanish and asking her to repeat them after him, explaining the grammar as he went along.

It seemed no time at all before he declared that that was enough for today, yet they had had a whole hour.

"Take the books with you," he said. "Try to *think* in Spanish, and from now on we will speak Spanish whenever possible."

"Shall I have a lesson tomorrow?" she asked.

"Oh yes, most certainly. Every day, if you wish. But I think we shall have to vary the times a little. Once you get into the swing of your work you might find it inconvenient to be here at stated times. You will, incidentally, be able to take your meals in whatever hotel you find yourself at meal times. Would you have any objection to sometimes having lessons in the evenings when you are off duty?"

"Of course not."

"Good. *Bueno*. But tomorrow, shall we say the same time? After we have seen the Botanical Gardens and had lunch I may show you more things, and by then it will be tea-time. After tomorrow you can get down seriously to work—*si*?"

"*Si*," she answered, gathering up the books.

Her brain a tangle of thoughts and impressions of the full and varied day, she went to her flat, and found when she went into the kitchen that someone had stocked the cupboard with all kinds of provisions. Tea, coffee, biscuits, sugar, preserves and various small tins of meat and fruit. In the small refrigerator was milk, cheese and butter—Juan's order without a doubt. A bowl of fresh fruit stood on a small table.

What a curious mixture of a man he was! Kind, painstaking, efficient, a man who did not like to be argued with, or at least, did not like his decisions to be questioned, she amended, remembering their discussion about modern hotels. In his work he could be something of a taskmaster, judging by their full programme today. But socially one could have very interesting conversations with him. And as a friend? One would need to know a little more about him. At present he was something of an enigma. He had made no mention of having parents, brothers or sisters and seemed to have no other home except the Hotel Marina. She had not known him for very long, of course, but surely long enough to know a little of his background. Perhaps he had had an unsuccessful marriage, her thoughts went on, and did not want to talk about it. Was that also why he had warded off Frasquita, because he had no wish to become involved seriously with a woman again?

The sight of her portfolio jerked her out of her speculations. Of what business of hers was Juan de Montserrat's private life? He was her employer and she was here to do a job of work.

She sat down and opened her portfolio.

CHAPTER FOUR

MARLENE stayed in her flat working on plans and designs until it was almost time for dinner. She changed into a dress which had been her father's favourite—a full-skirted one with black roses etched on a white background, and was slipping into her shoes when there came a knock on the door. She called out 'come in', expecting to see Micaela or even Juan himself. But to her surprise it was Ramon.

"*Buenas noches, señorita,*" he said with a broad smile.

"Oh—Ramon," she answered, too put out to respond to his Spanish. "You really shouldn't come in here, you know."

"But, *señorita*, you invited me in. I heard you distinctly!"

"You know perfectly well what I mean—and please don't sit down," she added swiftly as he seated himself in an armchair.

He immediately stood up again. "But what have I done to deserve such harsh treatment?" he asked, holding out both hands appealingly. "I'm simply mortified!"

"Don't be silly, you haven't done anything. It's just that I—have a feeling this sort of thing is frowned on in Spain."

He shrugged. "For Spanish girls, perhaps, but you are not Spanish. English girls are more—free, are they not?"

She opened the door. "I'm not quite sure what you mean by that, but I don't want to go against Spanish customs, and I have yet to find out Juan's feelings on the subject."

She must speak to him tonight about it, she determined as Ramon and she went down in the lift.

"Why did you come up to the flat?" she asked him, suddenly wondering whether he had been the bearer of a message from Juan, though this was hardly likely.

"To find you," he answered. "Frasquita said she hadn't seen you since about six o'clock."

"I've been busy. Juan took me to see his other hotels today and I wanted to do some planning while things were still fresh in my mind."

"Such industry! You shouldn't be working at all, a beautiful young lady like you."

She laughed. "What should I be doing?"

"You should be married."

"And I wouldn't then be working?"

"You would be looking after your husband and children."

"And that isn't work?"

He shrugged. "It is different. It is a woman's natural occupation."

He said it so seriously, she burst out laughing as they were stepping out of the lift. Juan was just passing and he turned his head sharply and gave them an unsmiling glance.

"There you are, you see," Ramon said. "He doesn't like anyone to laugh. But what *did* make you laugh? I didn't say anything funny."

For a moment, as she watched Juan's straight back, Marlene could not think why, either. Ramon put his hand under her elbow, taking it for granted, presumably, that she would accompany him to the cocktail bar. Her intention, before his arrival on the scene, had been to go into the staff room and read until time for dinner. But Juan turned in there, and she decided to wait for a little while.

"Not the cocktail bar. The lounge, please," she said to Ramon. "And if you really want to know, I was laughing at you. You sounded so terribly old-fashioned."

"Me? Old-fashioned? But what is old-fashioned about a woman looking after her own children? Don't you do that in England any more?"

"Of course we do. But sometimes a woman wants to carry on with her career. It may be important like being a doctor or—or an actress. Oh, any number of things."

"But when she marries, that is her career, just as a man chooses to work and earn money, not just for himself, but for his children also. Who is to look after the children if their mother is out working? Some other woman?"

By this time they were seated in the large lounge and Ramon had signalled a waiter, and when she looked around Juan was talking to one of the guests.

She did not really want to continue this discussion with Ramon. She was surprised that, as a young man, he still held these views about the place of women, but the fact that he did showed clearly the attitude which still existed towards them. If she argued with him from now until doomsday she would not convince him that a married woman could still have a career without necessarily neglecting her children. But she was not particularly anxious to convince him. She was never likely to marry him, so it did not matter to her what he thought.

He was determined to pursue the subject, however. "Well?" he demanded.

She laughed briefly. "You don't understand. Children grow up, spend most of their day at school. There are ways and means of keeping a career without neglecting children. In any case, some women don't have children."

"Nonsense!" he declared. "If a woman does not have children there is something wrong with her."

"Perhaps so."

"What about you?" he persisted. "Would you want to carry on with this—this garden job of yours if you married?"

"I might. But enough of this conversation, Ramon." Then she added as an afterthought, "I shall most likely marry an Englishman, anyway."

This seemed to surprise him. "Then why do you come to Spain?"

"I came for the sunshine," she told him, and added firmly: "And now, no more questions, because I shall refuse to answer them."

He gave her a calculating look and shook his head at her. "You are something of a mystery woman, Marlene, you know that? Why would a young and attractive young lady like you come all this way to do a job she was already doing in her own country?"

"I've told you, I'm answering no more questions. Let me ask you one. Why are you always here at the Hotel Marina?"

"Always? This is only the second night in succession. At first, I came to meet you because Frasquita asked me to. Tonight I come because I want to see you again and talk to you some more. Perhaps one evening you will come with me to Rosamar's—a nightclub in Lloret."

Marlene glanced at her watch and saw it was time to go along to Juan's dining room. She rose and asked Ramon to excuse her, hoping he had not been invited to dinner again. Out of courtesy he rose with her, and at that moment Frasquita approached them. She

67

looked upset about something.

"Juan is waiting for you," she said to Marlene. "Ramon and I are dining at home this evening."

"We are?" he asked in a tone of surprise.

"Yes," she said, tight-lipped and casting a look of sheer dislike at Marlene.

"I'd better go, then," she murmured, feeling distinctly uncomfortable. Clearly the girl was jealous. But why was she dining at home? Had Juan told her she must, and if so, why? Was there something special he wanted to talk to herself about, or was it because of his obvious dislike of Ramon? Perhaps whenever Ramon was in the hotel he felt obliged to ask him to dinner and two evenings in succession were too much.

Realizing with a little trepidation that this meant Juan and she would be dining alone together, she went into the room to find him listening to some music. She loved music herself, and the Beethoven Pastoral Symphony he was playing was one of her favourites.

He rose as she entered. "Is this music to your taste?" he asked almost at once.

"Very much so."

He crossed to the record player. "I'll turn the volume down, though, then we can talk."

Marlene sat down, wondering if there was something special he wanted to say to her. He offered her a drink and asked what she had been doing with herself since the Spanish lesson. When she told him he frowned.

"You mustn't work so hard. Why didn't you read a book or go for a walk—or even go to sleep?"

She laughed. "It's not like work to me. I love planning out gardens, deciding which plants would look well with others and so on. And there'll be plenty of time for walks, I imagine, in the summer. Or ought I to say spring?"

"Yes, you ought." His expression became clouded. "Were you working the whole of the time in your room?" he asked.

"Until I suddenly realized it was time to dress for dinner, yes," she told him.

There had been something odd in the way he had asked the question. Was he wondering how long Ramon had been in the flat? She determined to talk to him about it, but decided to wait until after they had eaten, as at that moment Micaela came in with the first course.

During the meal he asked her more about her life back home, and she found herself telling him about her broken engagement with Roger.

"It struck me there might be something else besides the death of your father," he said in a sympathetic tone of voice. "All in all, I think it was very brave of you to come away, and I think you're coping with your feelings very well indeed."

"I have an absorbing job. All the same, it—hurt at the time."

He nodded understandingly. "Are you still—"

"In love with him?" She shook her head. "I don't even think of him. I have other things now to—"

She broke off as Micaela came into the room again.

Juan gave her a penetrating look, and said: "Quite."

The word was loaded. Did he think Ramon had already taken Roger's place? She would have to put him right. She did not fall in and out of love as easily as all that. She noticed that, though he drew information out of her about her private life, he told her nothing of his. Perhaps he thought being her employer gave him the right. She decided to be bold and ask him a question.

"Where do your parents live, Juan?" she asked.

"I have no parents. So that puts us both in the same boat, as they say."

"I suppose it does." He did not volunteer any more information, but began to talk about Spain, by which she gathered that he did not want to talk about himself. She wondered why.

When they had finished their meal and Micaela had cleared away Juan offered Marlene a brandy. She accepted and they sat in silence for a few minutes listening to the music on the record player.

She cleared her throat. "Juan, there's something I want to talk to you about," she said.

"Yes? What is it? Nothing about work, I hope. If so, then it must wait until tomorrow."

"No," she answered quietly, "it isn't about work, but it's something I must get straight now—tonight."

"As urgent as that? Very well."

"It's—it's about the flat I'm occupying," she began.

"Something wrong with it?" he asked in a surprised voice.

"No, no. On the contrary. It's a lovely flat, very comfortable indeed. In fact, to digress for a moment, I understand it's actually *your* flat."

"Was," he corrected. "I chose to let you have it. The one I am occupying is quite adequate for my needs, so I beg you, no arguments about that," he said in a decisive tone.

"Very well, I won't. I can only say it was most kind of you, even though I don't feel entirely happy about it."

"Nonsense," he said crisply. "Please forget about it. Now, what was the other urgent matter you wanted to talk about?"

"I want to know how I stand about having visitors in the flat."

"You mean Ramon?" he asked sharply.

''No, no," she answered swiftly. "Not particularly, at any rate. But let's take Ramon as an example. How would you feel about his visiting the flat?"

He drew in a long breath. "If you want to entertain Ramon in your flat, that is entirely up to you. You must feel completely free to do as you please." He rose abruptly and, crossing to the record player, switched off the music. "Is that all you wished to say?" he asked stiffly.

It was clear that he was not pleased, in spite of what he had said about her feeling free.

Marlene shook her head. "No, Juan, it's not quite all," she said.

He had a look on his face which seemed to say he wanted to be gone, but she stood her ground.

"May I be honest with you?" she asked.

"By all means!"

"I have a feeling that you don't approve of Ramon. I mean—that you don't like him."

His lips tightened and his expression became dark. "Perhaps I don't, but my reasons are purely personal."

It was still not a very satisfactory answer. Perhaps she was not being quite honest enough.

"Juan, twice Ramon has visited my flat—not, I must emphasize, by invitation from me. But each time he has done so you've seen him and have looked displeased. I understand that, in Spain, women are regarded rather differently from those in my country. I have no wish to offend either you, personally, or against your customs. Above all, I have no wish to do anything to displease you."

She saw his face relax. He sat down again. "You are most considerate, and you are right when you say Spanish women are regarded differently. In Spain, a man must be manly and a woman must be feminine, a good home-maker and above all, chaste. An un-

71

married woman who risks her reputation does not have a very good chance of finding a husband. For that reason I am surprised that Ramon visited your flat—especially without your invitation. I shall speak to him about it."

"No, no, please don't. At least, not on my account."

His dark brows shot up. "Why not?"

"I expect he thought that Spanish customs didn't apply to me as I'm not Spanish."

"That is true. They do not. It depends on whether or not you want to settle down in this country. All the same, Ramon should have afforded the same respect and consideration towards you as he would to one of his countrywomen."

Marlene agreed with him, but she was more concerned with Juan's opinion than with Ramon's behaviour.

"What I really want to know is how you, personally, expect me to behave," she told him.

He thought for a moment, then said: "I would expect you to behave in the way which comes most natural to you. I am quite sure that you would not commit any terrible indiscretion. I want you to be free to entertain whom you wish in the flat. Regard it as your home. I will trust entirely to your own good taste. As to Ramon—tell me. Do you like him?"

She shrugged her shoulders. "I really can't give you a straight yes or no to that question. I don't *dis*like him. On the other hand—" She broke off. "Juan, if his presence annoys you or irks you—"

He gave a wry smile and shook his head. "He once did me an injury—claimed it was not his fault, of course. I'm not hanging on to an old feud or anything. He just seems to—what's the expression?—get under my skin. But he is the brother of Frasquita, so—"

"Yes, of course." He was prepared to put up with Ramon for her sake, it seemed.

"Tell me," Juan said suddenly, "what kind of things does Ramon talk to you about? I've seen you laughing together."

She smiled. "He certainly amused me tonight. But he wasn't really being funny. He was very serious—which for me made it more amusing."

"But why?"

"He was telling me, quite seriously, that a woman's place was in the home."

"And you found that amusing?"

"Only because it sounded so strange coming from the bright, gay, modern young man he had presented himself as being. He couldn't see that a woman should want a career outside the home at all. A married woman, that is."

Juan nodded. "It's the traditional Spanish outlook. When a woman marries she has chosen her career. Looking after the home, the husband and children is a full-time job."

She eyed him with interest. "So you hold those views, too?"

He inclined his head. "What man does not want to work for the woman he loves? He likes to think she is at home in the place which belongs to them both and that when he returns she will be there waiting for him."

"But suppose that is not what she wants to do?"

"Then she should not marry."

"She must give up the joys of a happy marriage just because she wants to carry on with what might be an important career?"

"A woman has to decide which is the most important to her."

"Ugh! How ruthless it sounds. Either—or."

73

"Life can be ruthless," he observed.

"It needn't be over something like this."

"My dear Marlene, it was you yourself who used the expression, not I. If you really loved a man you would not regard it in such terms."

He seemed to be winning the argument, for Marlene found herself in some agreement with him. All the same, she was not going to give in quite so easily.

"Perhaps not," she conceded. "But it does seem to me that it's the woman who is expected to do all the giving. Giving up a job she might want to keep, doing housework when her talents might lie elsewhere, staying at home alone all day while the children, if any, are at school, when she would much prefer to be among people."

He smiled. "We were talking about the Spanish way of life," he reminded her. "Spanish women accept the idea that their life is at home. Also the Spanish male is very jealous and possessive of his wife. If she went out to a place of work she might meet other men there and that could lead to disaster. In days gone by, if a married woman dishonoured her husband by having a relationship or love affair with another man she could be put to death. Such an extreme penalty does not happen today, of course, but the old traditions still discourage any tendency to flightiness."

"Very interesting. But in decent society the same goes in my country. Most couples, once married, are faithful to each other and don't want anyone else. But what about the Spanish male? He is jealous and possessive. Is he also chaste—or virtuous?"

Juan gave a slow smile. "He doesn't have to be. I mean, it isn't expected of him."

Marlene was outraged. "Well, that's a fine thing, I must say! And why, pray, should that be?"

74

"He has to prove his virility."

Marlene seethed. "In my country we have a saying: 'What's sauce for the goose is also sauce for the gander.'"

"There speaks the voice of the emancipated woman," Juan said with an amused smile.

"I will call it rather the voice of enlightenment," Marlene answered.

"Perhaps. But in my view there is much to be said for some of the old customs. Not all modern ideas are truly enlightened, by a long way."

She knew what he meant. She did not hold with the so-called permissive society of her own day and her own country, but there was also much of the Spanish attitude with regard to marriage and the place of women with which she could not possibly agree. Also, she found it hard to believe that Juan could be so backward in his thinking.

"And do you yourself subscribe to the idea that while a woman, married or single, should be virtuous, it's all right that a man is not?"

But he did not give her a direct answer. "We were talking about the Spanish custom, were we not? And to bring us back to the original point in question—it is for you to decide how closely to adhere to those customs. As far as the flat is concerned I want you to feel entirely free to entertain whom you please, just as you would in your cottage at home. Unless, of course, you think you might one day marry a man of this country. Then it might be advisable to—well, watch more carefully what you do."

Marlene put down her glass. "Whatever his nationality I would never marry any man unless he had the same views of fidelity after marriage—before, for that matter—as myself."

"Not even if you were deeply in love with him?"

She rose. "I hope I would never have the misfortune to fall in love with such a man, but if I did I also hope I'd have sufficient strength of mind not to marry him, because I could never be happy with him. Now, if you'll excuse me, I think I shall go to bed."

She thought she detected the glimmer of a smile hovering on his lips as he rose and opened the door for her.

"Sleep well, *señorita*. Don't forget we go to the Botanical Gardens in the morning."

Not entirely happy about all they had discussed, Marlene made her way up to the flat, heartily relieved that she did not see Ramon hovering about. She felt she had seen enough of the Spanish male for one evening. It troubled her, this role women were expected to play. Not every woman wanted to carry on with an outside career after marriage, but they should be free to choose without being condemned or forced to remain unmarried. It was so unfair.

She worried the thing for a while, then made herself shrug it off. She was here to do a job of work, and she would stay here for at least six months, but marry a man of this country? Never!

Blanes was bathed in sunshine for their visit to the Botanical Gardens of Carlos Faust. Juan drove there in his own car, along the bay past the statue of Joaquim Ruyra and up a steep hill to where the gardens were situated. The view of the bay from the top of the hill was simply magnificent, and Marlene would have lingered, but Juan led her away.

"We'll have plenty of time to look at the view during lunch. First, I want to show you a framed poem. It's written in Spanish, but I'll translate it for you. It's about trees, asking people to respect them for the many services they render to mankind."

The plaque was set on the Paseo Carlos Faust

76

leading to the gardens. It was headed: *Pasajero*. (To those who pass by.)

'I am the heat of your hearth during the cold
winter nights.
I am the friendly shade which you find when
you walk in the August sun.
My fruit quenches your thirst on the road.
I am the table in your house, the bed on
which you repose, the wood of your boat.
I am the handle of your spade, the door of
your dwelling, the wood of your cradle
and your coffin.
You who pass, hear me well, do me no
harm.'

"That's beautiful—all except the coffin bit," Marlene said. "What was it again? 'I am the heat of your hearth during the cold winter nights. I am the friendly shade which you find when you walk in the August sun'. I think it's lovely."

"I thought you would like it. I have a copy somewhere among my papers. I'll let you have it. It will help you with your Spanish, if nothing else," said Juan.

The trees and plants in the gardens were absolutely wonderful, a gardener's paradise. Marlene marvelled at the colours, the bougainvillaea still in bloom, the hibiscus, and the spiky aloe; the white-flowered yucca of Mexico, the exotic hechtia and the many giant cacti and stately Californian cypress and beautiful palm trees.

"One could spend all day in here!" she enthused as they stood beside a lake filled with aquatic plants, the blue Mediterranean in the background and to the right the Capuchin Monastery.

Juan smiled. "Well, you'll just have to come again

now you know where it is. There are over three thousand different species of plants here. You couldn't possibly see everything in one day, still less a half day."

They had lunch in the restaurant overlooking the bay and Marlene could scarcely eat for looking out of the window.

"You think you could be happy here in Blanes, then?" Juan asked her.

"Yes, oh yes! It's more beautiful than one could ever have imagined."

They had coffee at a little table outside where they could see the picturesque little temple dedicated to Linnaeus perched high on a rock, and far below, small rocky islands looking as if they had been thrown there by some giant hand. Marlene felt she wanted to sit here for ever.

"You seem entranced," Juan remarked after what must have been quite a long silence.

"I'm sorry." Marlene turned away from the view reluctantly. "You said this place—the bay and everything—was 'quite something', and you were right. In fact it was an understatement. But doesn't it ever rain here?"

He laughed. "Oh yes, it does indeed. Quite soon now we shall have some, and I only hope you will still find the bay enchanting."

"I expect it's like the English countryside. If you really like it you see beauty there whatever the weather."

"Even in your fogs—like the day I first came across you?"

Her face clouded for a moment at the recollection of that unhappy day, but her mind sought happier memories. "Yes, even in a fog the country can look beautiful. Trees and hedgerows look different, mysterious and remote, and everything is very silent."

"When you're happy and your heart is at peace, silence can be exquisite," Juan said softly. "But if the heart is troubled, silence can be full of voices and even the beating of your heart can be as thunder."

He seemed almost to be speaking to himself. Marlene was afraid to look at him in case she would be intruding on some personal and private experience.

In the silence a kind of spell somehow descended on them. She felt she had been privileged to catch a glimpse of the real man hidden by the hotel owner, the man of business, and she must pretend she had not heard what he had said, or had not fully understood, lest he should regret having revealed himself. But what he had said had been so full of insight and understanding, so absolutely true.

But a silence cannot go on for ever, and presently she sighed, sipped her coffee and smiled at him. "I could just sit here for always. Thank you so much for bringing me."

He nodded. "You've come a long way from home to work for me. I want you to settle down here for a while. You are going to be a great asset to the business."

Marlene noticed how swiftly he had steered away from the personal. She had never known a man whose moods could change so quickly.

"When is the greenhouse likely to be delivered?" she asked him. "I ought to be getting down to doing the job for which you're paying me."

He raised his eyebrows. "Such keenness! You've scarcely been here two days and you've already done quite a lot. The greenhouse should be delivered and erected tomorrow. It will be up to you to decide what form of heating you would like. In fact, you'd better make a list of all the things you are likely to require—

seed trays, growing media, seeds and so on—and they can all be delivered."

"Are there no shops in Blanes where I can go and buy such things? Especially flower seeds. I've brought a few with me, but—"

He shook his head. "Not that I am aware of. Home gardening is not the national pastime that it has evidently become in Britain. You have to go to the nurserymen. I must go into Barcelona this afternoon. Perhaps you should come with me. The flower stalls along the Ramblas will interest you. You could spend some time there—and look at the shops while I keep my business appointment. Then tomorrow you can start your practical work in earnest."

She did not argue with him. She had half made up her mind to spend the afternoon looking further around the Botanical Gardens, expecting that after lunch Juan would leave her to her own devices, but if he wanted her to see this Ramblas place—well, he was the boss.

"What is it? A sort of market place?" she asked.

He laughed. "No, no. It's a wide street or avenue. It runs right down to the harbour. Originally, it was the course of a stream which ran down from the mountains. I should think it's pretty unique in all the world. On either side there are shops, restaurants, theatres and so on. And in the centre there are trees, newspaper kiosks, the flower-sellers and something else besides. I won't tell you quite all, but there'll be more than enough to keep you interested for an hour or so.

Juan drove at some speed along the coast road, and Marlene found it an exhilarating experience. He drove in silence, which gave her time for reflection on the nature and personality of the man for whom she had come to Spain to work. He had so many facets to his character as to be bewildering at times. But one thing she had observed above all others was that, as soon as any conversation became personal, he changed the subject. Yet he was kind, even though he did not like to be argued with. She was enjoying being taken around by him, but she told herself that he was doing this only because she was strange to the country—a foreigner. After today she would no doubt be left very much to her own devices, especially as he had provided her with her own transport.

Barcelona was an absolutely thrilling place. Juan drove past the impressive statue of Christopher Columbus, and by a series of twists and turns along the great Avenue of Generalisimo Franco which virtually cut the city in half. They passed a bullring, and Marlene gave an involuntary shudder.

Juan glanced at her and gave a wry smile. "You have the Britisher's automatic aversion to the sport—and yet it is the tourists who have given bullfighting its boost."

"You have other tourists beside the British," she answered defensively.

"True, but your people do come here in great numbers, and considering they have a reputation for being animal-lovers—"

"I expect they go out of curiosity, just to be able to go home and say they've seen a bullfight."

"And shudder in the telling?"

"I expect so."

"Would you like to see a bullfight?" he asked.

"No," she said emphatically. "Definitely not, even out of curiosity. Do you go often?"

To her surprise he shook his head. "No, I don't go."

He offered no reason and she let the subject drop. But surely it was unusual for a Spaniard not to like bullfighting? Or *were* there some who didn't? Not quite everyone in her own country was a fanatic about football and cricket, for instance.

But soon all these kind of speculations went out of her head. Juan parked the car and after a short walk they were in that most fascinating of all places in Barcelona, the Ramblas.

"Here you are," said Juan. "Local colour, people of all ages, classes—as well as nationalities. Shops, flowers, atmosphere. I shall leave you now to keep my business appointment, and when I've finished I shall come and find you."

He disappeared, and Marlene looked all around her. It was a most gay and exciting sight; people walking at leisure looking happy, no cars rushing up and down, and a little way from where she was standing vivid banks of flowers. At this moment the shops were not for her. She walked towards the flowers as though drawn by a magnet. There were roses, carnations, dahlias, chrysanthemums, tall plumes of pampas grass and masses of everlasting flowers. And all were arranged artistically in tiers to form banks of colour which were a sheer delight. Not only that, but there were separate flower arrangements, some consisting entirely of everlasting flowers such as the statice suworowi and perezii, the dainty acroclinium, the showy helichrysum and many others mixed with dried grasses of all kinds. They were the flower-arranger's dream.

Marlene wished she had someone with her so that she could keep exclaiming how beautiful. She went slowly up one side and down the other, feasting her eyes on the many lovely blooms. She would make Juan's gardens a joy to look at. In sheltered places and where it could be best admired she would even have the exotic strelitza, the Bird of Paradise flower.

Then suddenly she came across the bird-sellers. This

was what Juan had not told her about. Marlene stood watching the bright, colourful creatures and marvelled at them—the yellow canaries, the budgerigars, the tiny humming birds in special glass aviaries for extra warmth and so many of which she did not know the names. Keeping birds in cages had never appealed to her, but she could not help admiring them and taking pleasure in them.

"Like one for your room?" said a voice behind her.

She swung around to see Juan. "No, no," she answered with a shake of her head. "They're delightful to watch for a little while, but I prefer to see them with more room in which to fly free."

He nodded and led her back to the flower-sellers where he bought a bouquet of flowers and presented them to her.

"This is something you will like, I know."

"For me?" she said in delighted surprise. "They're beautiful. How charming of you!"

He gave an amused smile. "I must admit I'm seldom called 'charming'. Have you seen all you want to see along the Ramblas? The shops and everything?"

She laughed. "I haven't been anywhere near the shops. You've scarcely been gone half an hour."

"An hour and a quarter," he corrected. "Well, we might as well make a day of it. I have to get back to the hotel in time for the guests' evening meal, but we have time for tea and to look at some of the shops."

What an extraordinary person he was, she reflected as he led her past what looked like a group of business men talking and gesticulating amiably. An extraordinary man in rather an extraordinary country.

The shops were wonderful. There was beautiful silverware polished to a brilliant shine under the shop window lighting; magnificent jewellery which almost took one's breath away—as did the prices; the leather goods were fascinating in their quality and variation and the porcelain was a dream in beauty and elegance. Juan pressed her to say what she liked and disliked, although of the latter there was very little.

"All you need is lots of money," she said with a sigh.

"If you had a great deal of money, what sort of things would be on the top of your list?" Juan asked her.

"Oh dear—what a difficult choice!"

"Really? I would have thought you might fancy some particular piece of jewellery."

She considered for a moment. "Well, no, not really. If I had a great many evening engagements and I wanted a piece of jewellery to wear with a certain dress or dresses, then it would be nice to be able to choose something which really suited the item no matter how expensive, but I wouldn't just buy jewellery for the sake of buying it. I think on the whole I'd put a piece of porcelain on the top of my shopping list."

"A good choice. And silver?"

"If I were setting up a home, yes."

"And what about clothes?" he queried as they halted outside a shop with a very high fashion look.

Marlene laughed. "Like most women, that's where I would be the most extravagant."

"And rightly so," he approved. "A beautiful woman should always be well dressed."

Marlene's eyes widened. Was that intended as a personal compliment, or was he generalizing? She decided it must be the latter. After all, such compliments were usually made in an atmosphere of soft lights and music, and in a low, soft voice, not out on a pavement in a voice so matter-of-fact. She felt she couldn't let his remark go unanswered, however, so she decided to treat the matter as a joke.

"And what about a handsome man?"

He nodded. "The same. While it is true that *el habito no hace al monje*—the dress does not make the man—a well-dressed man can inspire confidence and respect."

After this, Juan took her to a restaurant where he knew they could be served with tea, and Marlene found a sort of contentment settling upon her.

She sighed, "It will be down to earth with a bump for me tomorrow."

"Why so?" he queried.

"All these pleasurable outings. I've come here to work."

"Say rather that you have come here to *live*."

She laughed. "Well, I must say you're breaking me in gently!"

"I have been showing you where the places of work are, and you have not been idle by any means."

His appreciation of her efforts added to her feeling of contentment, and when at last they arrived back at the Hotel Marina she felt happier than she had ever thought possible. It had been a wonderful day.

Frasquita was in the reception area of the hotel when Juan and Marlene entered.

"Marlene, there is a letter for you in the office," the girl said, her dark gaze sliding past Marlene to Juan.

Marlene thanked her and went to get it. It was postmarked England and was in Brenda's handwriting. Eager to have news of her friends, Marlene tore open the envelope as she went up in the lift to her flat. It was a long letter. Marlene turned to the back page where there was a lengthy postscript and one sentence stood out from the rest.

Roger, you may not be surprised to hear, is not to marry Caroline, after all. She—

CHAPTER FIVE

MARLENE drew in her breath sharply and the hand holding the letter fell to her side. Her mind a confusion of thoughts, she entered her room and sat down weakly in a chair. So the break between Roger and herself, the heartache, her coming to Spain—all had been in vain. For a minute or two the painful past came back in a rush, everything happening again. She could have stayed in England, after all. Roger and herself might well have—

But suddenly she brought herself up sharply. What was she about, thinking this way? She must be mad. Surely she wasn't still in love with Roger? She couldn't be. It was just the shock of learning the news, that was all.

She looked at the letter again. The postscript went on: *She says she's broken it off. He says he has. So which of them are you to believe? I think Roger has discovered that she's not so wealthy, after all, and maybe SHE has found out that he was only marrying her for the money he thought she had. It's my belief Roger wishes now that he hadn't broken with you. He wants your address. Shall I let him have it? Brenda.*

Marlene stared into space, her mind for a while having difficulty in absorbing the implications of this news. Was Brenda's surmise correct, and was Roger now regretting their own broken engagement? At any rate he wanted her address. Putting off coming to a decision or examining her heart further for the time being, Marlene read the rest of Brenda's letter. It was full of small items of news about Brenda herself and Molly, and various other mutual friends. Marlene felt the beginnings of homesickness creeping over her. It was good to have friends like Brenda and Molly. She missed them. If only she had similar friends here. Perhaps, in time, Frasquita and herself would become better acquainted. At present, Marlene found it difficult to get through to her.

She sighed, and in one sense wished the letter had not come. It had unsettled her. She had had a lovely day with Juan, and until she had read the letter had been feeling happy and contented. Now the past had come back to haunt her and fill her with uncertainties. She had thought herself completely out of love with Roger, but obviously one did not fall out of love quite so easily. If Roger now wanted to marry her, would she accept?

She had her bath and dressed for the evening, then picked up her Spanish books and went downstairs. Juan was waiting for her.

"I'm afraid I haven't made much progress," she told him ruefully.

He smiled. "You could hardly be expected to as you've been out all day, but once you start going about your work and trying to converse with the staff and the people who serve you in the shops, you will find it will begin to come to you. For the moment let us go over the first lesson again. You may be surprised to discover how much you know already."

Marlene found it difficult to concentrate fully, however, and it was not very long before Juan told her to close the books.

"You've had a full day and certainly no time for a *siesta*," he said.

"It's been a lovely day," she answered, and found she was beginning to relax again in his company.

He poured her a drink and eyed her keenly.

"Frasquita tells me you had a letter from England. Was it good news from friends?"

She wished he had not asked her. Feeling the need to talk to someone, she was almost tempted to tell him about Roger. She took a deep breath and forced a smile.

"Just—ordinary news about everyday things and people."

There was a short silence, then he said: "If you want at any time to invite friends to stay with you, do feel free to do so. There are a couple of rooms on the same floor as your flat which I usually keep empty for just such a purpose. Your friends could have the use of your flat and the dining room during the day."

"That's very generous of you. I'll tell Brenda and Molly. I'm sure they'd love to come."

He nodded. "We must keep you happy or my plans for beautifying the hotels will go awry. You're bound to miss your friends from time to time. I must look up my English acquaintances here and introduce you to a few people."

She noticed that he did not mention Frasquita as being a possible friend. Was he well aware of how she felt about him and her jealousy of any other woman?

Juan was silent for a few minutes, then he said suddenly: "I have to go away for a few days, and may be gone before you come down in the morning. Is there anything you wish to discuss about the work before I go?"

"I can't think of anything at the moment. The greenhouse will be delivered tomorrow?"

He nodded. "You will have plenty with which to occupy yourself for a few days, and I have no doubt that Ramon will be on hand to take care of your evenings. But beware of that young man and do not

88

take too seriously anything he might say of—a personal nature." Then he said more lightly : "Above all, do not get lost, and remember to drive on the right-side of the road."

She was tempted to take issue with him with regard to Ramon taking care of her evenings, but she restrained herself. She contented herself by thanking him, and then Frasquita came into the room and dinner was served.

It was odd not seeing Juan the next day. Marlene missed him strangely. She attended to the plants in the two hotels in Blanes, then drove to Pineda to supervise the erecting of the greenhouse and to choose the form of heating she wanted. She had discussed this with Juan earlier and he had reminded her that Spain was a large country compared with England and that there were even greater variations in climate than there.

"While it is hot here in the summer, we are in the north of the country and we can and do have cold weather in late February and March. You have to remember, too, that we are between the mountains and the sea."

She certainly found, as she watched the greenhouse being erected, that though the sun was shining there was a cold wind blowing from the mountains. When the sun clouded over or it rained some heat would certainly be needed for the raising of plants from seed or for tender cuttings. Bearing these facts in mind and also an imminent war in the Middle East with threatened oil shortages, she decided to have both electric and oil heating, each with thermostatic control for cold nights and other variations of temperature. The electric heating she could use immediately, and this she did. Before nightfall she had a most satisfactory array of cuttings snug and warm in the greenhouse.

That evening she stayed in her room until it was time for dinner. She switched on television and listened to the news and other items which, though she could only pick up a word now and then that she understood, was at least getting her accustomed to hearing the Spanish language. When the programme turned to music she picked up her books and attempted the first written exercise. She must show some progress by the time Juan returned.

She was not surprised that Ramon had been invited to dine with Frasquita and herself. What was surprising to her was the extraordinary devotion of the brother and sister, even allowing for the strong family ties of the Spanish.

"Where have you been hiding yourself all evening?" Ramon asked when she entered the room.

"All evening?" she queried. "I thought the evening was only just beginning in Spain?"

"True, but as your customs differ a little I looked for you earlier."

"That's very kind of you, but I was busy in my room."

Here Frasquita intervened. "Juan told me to see to it that you did not work too hard, Marlene. What were you doing up there?"

"Learning my Spanish."

Ramon frowned and pulled a face. "What a waste! You do much better to come and talk to me—and I could talk to you in Spanish. If I had known I would have ventured to come up to your flat—or am I to be barred for always?"

Marlene eyed him squarely. "Tell me, Ramon, if I were a Spanish girl would you expect to come into my flat with no one else present except ourselves?"

He shrugged. "Perhaps not, but you are different.

You are English and you have no family here to—well, interfere."

"And what about my reputation?"

"But who is here to see?"

"The staff. Besides, what would *you* think of me if I gave you the freedom of my flat?"

"I would think you O.K. Many of our customs are —what you say—old hat, anyhow."

Marlene laughed. "That isn't the impression you gave me the other evening."

Frasquita leaned forward and touched her arm in her first really friendly gesture.

"Marlene, apart from Juan, my brother and I are the only people you know here. Please regard us both as your friends—even your 'family'. It would be all right for Ramon to visit your flat. There would be no harm."

Marlene was touched. "Thank you, Frasquita. Thank you very much indeed. Perhaps both you and Ramon would let me give you coffee in my room some time."

"That would be fine," Ramon said swiftly.

When they had eaten Ramon asked her if she would like to go to one of Blanes' *bodegas*.

"Will Frasquita come too?" she asked.

Frasquita shook her head. "When Juan is away I stay on duty. I sleep here. You and Ramon go. It will be all right."

Marlene decided she had better stop worrying about proprieties, and so she went upstairs to get a coat.

"What is a *bodega*?" she asked Ramon as they stepped outside.

"You will see. It is a place where you can sit and drink Spanish wine in convivial company. You will hear only Spanish spoken."

"No tourists?"

"Not usually in the one I shall take you to. Perhaps they cannot find it. It is known only to local people. And to tell the truth I am glad to get out of Juan's hotel."

"Why do you go there if you don't like it?" she asked.

His shoulders lifted. "For my sister's sake."

Marlene did not quite understand. Did he feel Frasquita needed chaperoning when Juan was in residence? It hardly made sense.

"To tell you the truth," Ramon went on, "I don't like my sister working for Montserrat."

"Oh? But why? He seems to me a very good person for whom to work."

"You have found him so, I daresay, but you have only been here a few days."

Marlene did not like this conversation. What Ramon had said was true, but the implication that Juan was a difficult man to work for she simply did not believe. Then she thought of the times he had spoken sharply when she had ventured to question a decision he had made.

"All the same, Ramon, I would rather not discuss Juan in his absence," she said.

"Why not?"

"It's a question of loyalty, I suppose."

"I have a loyalty, too—to my sister. She will hate me for saying this, but she is in love with Juan. He led her on, now he treats her abominably."

"That's not true."

"It is so. Frasquita has pain in her heart all the time."

"But that's hardly Juan's fault," Marlene protested.

"No, *señorita*, perhaps not. Perhaps it is your fault."

"My fault!" Marlene stopped short. This conversation was getting quite out of hand. "I really think I shall go back to the hotel."

"No, no, Marlene—please. I am sorry. It is just that I hate to see my sister so hurt, and I was hoping you might be able to help."

"But how can I help?"

"To the *bodega*, Marlene, then we can talk. It will not yet be crowded."

Only because she herself had seen Frasquita's unhappiness and her jealousy did Marlene consent to going with him. She also knew only too well the pain and desolation of rejection.

Ramon led her by a series of left and right turns in narrow streets to a place called the Bodega el Toro.

"The bull, of course," Ramon informed her.

They entered by a door which creaked on its hinges and was in danger of dropping off. The interior was gloomy and cellar-like, and at first Marlene did not like it very much. Ramon shook hands with the proprietor and greeted a number of friends in the same way as he led her to a quiet corner. While he ordered drinks for them both she looked about her, her eyes becoming accustomed to the gloom.

The colourwashed brick walls were covered with fishing nets in a bluey-green colour and caught here and there with dried flowers which looked as if they had been hanging there for centuries. Along one end of the place were great and small casks of wine— Jerez, Rosado Toro, Misa, Jumilla, Porto, and so on. The tables and stools were of rough, natural wood and around the room were one or two plants looking, Marlene considered, in quite good condition in the circumstances. Obviously somebody cared for them, and she began to like the place a little more.

Ramon sipped his drink in silence for a minute or two, then he leaned towards her.

"*Señorita*—" he began earnestly, "I speak only of

these things because of the love I have in my heart for my sister, believe me. I wish only that she did not love this man. He is not good for her. I do not like him and he does not like me. When she first went to work for him he was kind to her, as he is now to you, and she lost her heart to him. Soon he changed towards her. Every now and again he goes on these mysterious trips of his to the mountains. Why? Who knows? Maybe he has some mountain retreat where he keeps a wife. I do not know. Nobody knows. And then you come along and—" he lifted his shoulders and gave a despairing gesture, "now my sister is more unhappy than ever."

Marlene scarcely knew what to say. "But—but, Ramon, unless Juan told Frasquita that he loved her—"

"A man does not always have to say these things."

She shook her head. "You're wrong, Ramon. A man can be kind to a woman without being in love with her. I—I would never take it for granted that a man loved me simply because he was kind. I'd want to hear him say it." *And even then he didn't always mean it,* she thought with sudden bitterness.

Ramon gave her a keen look. "You are not, then, in love with Juan yourself?"

Marlene stared at him in blank surprise, then tossed back her head and laughed outright.

"Good heavens, Ramon, you've got love on the brain! How could I possibly be in love with Juan? I've known him barely a week."

"So what? There is such a thing as love at first sight."

"True, but it didn't happen to me, I assure you."

"It could have happened to Juan."

She sighed and shook her head. "That's an even sillier remark."

"Then why did he ask you to come here, just like that?"

"He saw me at work and liked what I was doing."

"And was that the first time you had met?" She told him it was, and explained to him where she worked.

"But what was Montserrat doing there?"

"How on earth should I know? All I do know is that he had some business or other with Lord Hetherington. He was interested in plants, came to look around, saw me, offered me a job—or at least, he did later on, and I accepted simply because he made Blanes sound attractive. Also, my father had recently died, I have no other special ties, just friends, and if that isn't enough it was a cold, foggy day and 'sunny Spain' sounded inviting. Juan was very businesslike about the whole thing, I assure you."

Ramon frowned a little, then he brightened. "All right, I'll take your word for it. Perhaps, then, you will be willing to help Frasquita."

"I will if I can, but I don't see how."

"Simple. Just try to leave Juan and Frasquita together more."

Marlene laughed briefly. "You know, you've exaggerated things enormously. Juan has only been showing me around his hotels—necessary, you must admit, since my work will take me to all of them."

"And the trip to the Botanical Gardens and Barcelona? Were they necessary?" he queried.

Marlene was beginning to feel he was bordering on the impertinent, but she answered: "I promise you, I shall be extremely busy from now on, so I don't expect to see much of Juan myself—except at meal times, that sort of thing."

"I'm glad to hear it," he said. "Perhaps you will come out to dinner with me. That will be one way of

95

leaving them together sometimes. And because it will be a pleasure and an honour to take out such a lovely lady as yourself," he added as if on an afterthought.

Marlene laughed good-humouredly. "Well, perhaps I will, but don't expect too much. Juan is giving me Spanish lessons for an hour several evenings a week."

"So unnecessary!" declared Ramon.

But Marlene felt she had taken enough. "I'll remember what you have said, Ramon, and I'll do my best, but Juan is the boss, after all, don't forget. I feel for your sister—very much indeed, but neither your scheming nor anyone else's will make Juan fall in love with her. Quite honestly, if I were in her shoes I would find another job."

"That is what I have told her, time and time again! But she refuses to listen. She would rather suffer and go on hoping. So undignified."

"Ramon, love and dignity seldom go hand in hand."

"But you'll help? Frasquita was just beginning to hope at last when you came. Now—"

"I've already told you, Ramon. She has absolutely no rival in me. However, I'll do my best to help things along. You men are often very blind and don't see what is under your noses, clever enough though you might be in other directions. And now, let us drop the subject."

The *bodega* was filling up rapidly. Sometimes young men would come in together, at others whole groups of mixed sexes would burst in. Girls, she noticed, never came in together. What happened? Did they stroll up and down the sea-front in groups until they met their counterparts, then by common consent enter the *bodega*?

The atmosphere became thick with smoke and very lively. A guitar was produced and there was singing, then one of the girls produced a flounced skirt which she slipped over her shoulders and slid on to her waist. She began to dance, and the guitar music became more passionate and intense. The girl who, minutes before, had been laughing and talking with her friends had now become a different person, haughty and aloof, and she danced in a small area which had been formed for her.

"Is she dancing the *flamenco*?" whispered Marlene.

Ramon shook his head. "No, no. It is just a Spanish folk dance—España Cañi. But she hopes to dance the *flamenco* one day. For the true *flamenco* you have to go somewhere like Rosamars in Lloret. I'll take you some time."

She would have answered that Juan had already mentioned taking her there, but the company had started a rhythmic hand-clapping to the beat of the music and further conversation was impossible.

It was well past midnight when Ramon took her back to the hotel, and this he considered early.

As she feared he might, he mentioned again taking her to see the *flamenco* at Rosamars.

"But we will wait until Juan is back, I think. This would give Frasquita her chance."

"I'm sorry, Ramon, but Juan offered to take me. When I've first been with him, then perhaps—"

Ramon drew in a furious breath and his dark eyes gleamed. "Juan—Juan, I could sometimes kill him!" he muttered angrily, shaking two tightly clenched fists.

"For goodness' sake, Ramon, stop getting so worked up about Juan and everything! If you go on like this I shall simply have to have nothing more to do with you. Juan is now my boss and I owe him a measure of loyalty. If, as time passes, he doesn't mention taking me to see the *flamenco* again, well, then I'll take it that he wasn't really issuing a firm invitation and accept yours—if you should ask me again. For the rest, my work and learning the language is going to take up most of my time, and so I don't expect to see much of Juan except in the line of my work. I am certainly no rival to Frasquita."

At this she bade him a firm goodnight and escaped to the calm privacy of her flat.

For a long time, however, she could not get all the things Ramon had said out of her mind. She had not been in the country more than the proverbial five minutes, and already, it seemed, she was involved in a feud between her boss and another man, and being virtually accused of causing a rift in a love affair. About the feud, whatever its cause, she could do nothing, though it certainly existed between the two men, as she had observed herself. And about Frasquita? Was it possible that, with a little encouragement, he might fall in love with her as she undoubtedly was with him? While it was true that love could not be forced, a gentle push often made a person stumble on the truth. Perhaps a previous unsuccessful love affair had made Juan cautious, as in her own case.

This thought sent her mind in the direction of Roger, and Brenda's letter. Incidents from the past came floating by to be re-lived and re-assessed. Then for some strange reason she found herself comparing Roger with Juan and could almost have laughed at the absurdity. There simply *was* no comparison. In manliness, dignity, kindness and general stature Roger never would, or could, measure up to a man like Juan.

In acknowledging this she knew quite definitely that she could never marry Roger, even if he asked her. She no longer loved him.

With some relief at this decision she slid between the sheets, and a feeling of contentment stole over her.

She was going to be happy here working for Juan. Very, very happy.

She was drifting off to sleep when suddenly she sat bolt upright. If she were not careful she would be falling in love with Juan herself. She was beginning to admire him too much, to feel too happy in his company. She took a deep breath and compressed her lips determinedly. She mustn't. She did not want to fall in love again so soon—it was too painful. She must do all she could to prevent such a thing happening. To fall in love with a man like Juan could be disastrous. Frasquita was the woman he should marry. She was his kind, his nationality. Marlene herself must spend as little time in his company as possible. After all, there was no reason why she should spend any time at all with him except in working hours, and on his return she would suggest giving up having Spanish lessons with him. She would tell him that she preferred to study on her own. One thing she could do was go to the local cinemas, and she could also spend more evenings listening to and watching television. She simply must not fall in love with him.

Juan was away for a full three days. Marlene pondered once or twice over what Ramon had said about Juan's 'mountain retreat'. Was he, in fact, visiting a woman he loved, and for some reason known only to himself preferred that no one should know of it?

The weather had suddenly turned much colder and dark rain clouds now covered the sun. There was news of heavy rainfall in the south and opinion was that any day now the north-east coast would have its share. Marlene moved the more tender plants indoors, some in her greenhouse, others in different parts of the appropriate hotels. Additional packets of flower seeds she had decided to ask Brenda to send her from home.

She was surprised to find how much she missed Juan. At first she couldn't quite place her strange lost feeling, of things being not quite right, a kind of incompleteness, and she discovered that whatever she did, thoughts of him were there, lingering at the back of her mind. Or, more to the forefront, wondering what he was doing, who he was visiting in the mountains.

It occurred to her that he bore the same name as the nearby range of mountains called Montserrat, meaning 'saw-tooth mountain' because of the large peaks which were silhouetted against the skyline, information she had gleaned from an excursion leaflet given her by an English guest. Had Juan been born in the mountains? she wondered. In English his name was John of Montserrat, or John of the saw-tooth mountain.

But she was letting her imagination run away with her. She had once known someone called Derbyshire who certainly had not been born in that county, and strictly speaking she had only Ramon's word that Juan had gone to a mountain retreat. Juan himself had not said where he was going, and it was no business of either hers or anyone else's to speculate. And why was he so much in her mind? She told herself it was because of his strong personality. Also, at present, he was the one person in this strange country to whom she felt closest, that was all. She certainly did not feel any real affinity for Ramon, and Frasquita consistently held herself aloof. Juan had promised to introduce her to some English friends of his. From those she hoped to make friends of her own.

She answered Brenda's letter, giving her a detailed description of Blanes and the lovely bay, the Botanical Gardens and of her trip to Barcelona with Juan.

"It's all turning out wonderfully," she told her.

"Juan—we all use first names—is a wonderful person to work for. He has given me a free hand, provided me with a little greenhouse, and I have a lovely little flat overlooking this absolutely marvellous bay. He has said I can have friends to stay any time I like, so please come—and Molly—as soon as you can get some time off. As to Roger, I'm sorry his marriage to Caroline didn't come to anything after all, but for my part I've got him out of my system completely now. I have a new life here and I'm happy. I'm learning the language and getting to know the people and might even settle down here for good." She signed her name with a sigh of satisfaction.

After dinner on a day she invited Frasquita and Ramon to her flat for coffee Marlene went upstairs to make it, leaving the other two to follow a little later. Her percolator was bubbling nicely when a knock came at the door, but to her surprise only Ramon stood there.

"Frasquita will be up directly," he said, smiling broadly. "She was on her way when she was hailed by a customer. May I enter your holy of holies?"

"She'd better be here soon," Marlene answered, stepping aside so that he could enter. "Otherwise out you go."

"Why? Don't you trust me?"

"It isn't a question of not trusting you," she retorted. "I don't want to offend against Spanish customs. You know the saying: When in Rome—"

"That's ridiculous!"

"Ridiculous or not, you're getting no coffee until your sister puts in an appearance."

He pulled a face and shrugged. "As a matter of fact, she *did* tell me to tell you not to wait for her in case she was delayed longer than she expected."

"A likely story," Marlene said derisively. But she

was not terribly serious. She invited him to take a seat and sat down opposite to him. "All right, then. Speak to me in Spanish. *Yo deseo hablar español.*"

Ramon groaned, "Oh, no! Must we?" then added, in a stilted voice: "*Como esta usted? Estoy muy bien, gracias. Y usted?*"

"Really, Ramon! That's too elementary even for me."

"All right. How is this?"

He came out with a long string of words in rapid Spanish she could not possibly understand except a word here and there.

"I'm sure what you said is very interesting," she retorted, "but you know perfectly well I'm not as advanced as all that. What was it you said?"

"I said evenings are for leisure, not for learning. Here we are, an attractive woman, a handsome man —if I may say so—and you want to learn to speak a foreign language. It will come, my dear, it will come. Why don't you relax and enjoy yourself?"

But somehow Marlene did not feel very relaxed in his company. She did not know why, unless it was because he did not like Juan. Whatever it was, she felt uneasy, and wished Frasquita would come, though conversation between the three of them never seemed to flow very easily.

As she did not speak for a minute or two Ramon spoke again. "All right, tell me about your life in England, then I'll help you with your Spanish, eh?"

Marlene did not very much want to talk about England, but it would pass the time until Frasquita came, so she told him about the estate, how beautiful it was in the summer—the smooth, undulating green lawns, the great trees, the early morning mists of autumn, the russet and gold tints which came at the first touch of frost.

"And in the winter?" queried Ramon as she paused.

"Even in winter it can be beautiful, especially when the larch and spruce are heavy with snow—"

"And food has to be dropped to the people in your villages by helicopter."

"That is a rare, not a usual occurrence," she told him.

"Of course. I'm only joking. Now, what about this Spanish? Let me see what you've done so far." As he spoke he glanced at his watch. "I wonder what is keeping Frasquita? Would you like me to go down and see what's happening?"

Marlene accepted this suggestion with relief, but he was gone only a few minutes.

"Some difficult guests," he explained. "She will be up as soon as she possibly can."

Marlene was studying some Spanish vocabulary, so Ramon brought his chair close to hers. There was dialogue also in the book and Ramon suggested they should each read a part and he would correct her pronunciation as they went along. Marlene became quite absorbed, so did not know how long it was before a knock came at the door.

"Ah, Frasquita at last," she said, and called out to her to come in.

But it was not Frasquita who entered. It was Juan, his face dark with anger.

CHAPTER SIX

FOR a moment Marlene simply stared at him, then, as she realized what an intimate picture Ramon and she must make, she leapt to her feet.

"Juan, how—how nice to see you back! Ramon was helping me with my Spanish while—"

He did not wait to hear the rest, but went out again, closing the door behind him. Marlene ran across the room.

"Let him go—" muttered Ramon.

But she wrenched open the door and stepped out into the corridor in time to see Juan inserting the key in the lock of his own apartment.

"Juan, please! We were waiting for Frasquita to join us for coffee."

He turned and looked at her, and though his features had now relaxed a little his face still looked stern.

"I see. Well, I'll see you in the morning, Marlene."

"Is there something you wished to see me about tonight?" she asked, feeling strongly that he was still displeased about seeing Ramon in her room. "Or—or can I offer you coffee?"

He opened his door. "Thank you, but no. Goodnight."

She had no option but to return to her room. Ramon was seated where she had left him, grinning broadly.

"I think we'd better not wait for Frasquita," Marlene said, fighting down her irritation with him. "We'll have our coffee now."

Ramon rose and followed her into the kitchen. "Wasn't it rich—the look on his face?" he said with a laugh.

"I don't see anything rich about it," she told him. "I'm sorry, Ramon, but I really don't think you'd better come to the flat any more. Juan did say I had complete freedom, that I could invite whom I wished, but it's quite obvious he has some objection to you."

"Maybe he's jealous."

"Don't be silly. Why should he be? Perhaps he doesn't like Spanish customs being violated, after all."

She thought it was much more likely to be something personal between the two men, some old feud, but she kept this thought to herself.

The coffee now ready, she carried in the tray. As soon as she had fulfilled this one social obligation, she would ask Ramon politely to leave, she decided. Why Frasquita had been delayed for so long, she could not think. After dinner had been served to the guests there was not usually any demand on their services.

About five minutes later, Frasquita arrived. She apologized for keeping them waiting.

Ramon gave a smile of amusement. "I suppose you knew Juan was back?"

She nodded. "He arrived about ten minutes ago." The girl avoided looking at Marlene, who had a sudden suspicious thought.

"Did you know he was coming back tonight, Frasquita?" she asked.

Frasquita's dark eyes widened and she shook her head vigorously. It was Ramon who answered.

"He never does let anyone know when he's coming back from these trips of his. I think he does it deliberately to see if the 'mice are playing' while he is away. As he maybe thinks he did tonight."

"Ramon—*please*," entreated his sister.

"Sorry," he said smoothly.

Frasquita sipped her coffee in brooding silence. Marlene could not help feeling sorry for the girl, and she reflected that her brother's attitude hardly helped the situation, in spite of his supposedly deep concern.

"Did Juan say whether or not he had had a good trip?" she asked her.

Frasquita put down her cup and rose. "I think he always has a good trip, but he never talks about it," she answered. "Thank you for the coffee, Marlene. I must go now, and I'd like to go home, Ramon, if you don't mind."

This was Marlene's opportunity to make sure that Ramon really did leave. She rose to her feet, also, leaving him with no option but to do the same.

"I think I'll have an early night, too, though by my standards it's quite late already," she said, glancing at her watch and noting that it was eleven o'clock.

"Oh, I'd thought of coming back for another coffee," said Ramon, blatantly ignoring her hint. He grinned broadly. "You don't have to get up early in the morning to milk the cows, you know."

"Frasquita can make you another cup of coffee when you get home," Marlene told him firmly. "Thank you both for coming. Good night."

"*Hasta la vista*," Ramon murmured in her ear as he went out.

Marlene closed the door behind them and gave a sigh of relief. Never again would she invite Ramon into her flat and risk Juan's displeasure. She tried to see the scene through his eyes as he had entered her room. There had sat a man, in what was, after all, his flat, whom he thoroughly disliked. It must have given him quite a shock. What was it between the two? she wondered.

She made her preparations for bed feeling a strange

contentment that Juan was back again. The place had not been the same without him. It was nice to think that he was once more in the room next to hers.

Marlene was surprised to find how lighthearted she was the next morning. She made her way downstairs after breakfasting in her room hoping to see him and explain further about Ramon being in her room last night. But to her great disappointment he had already gone out.

"Did you want to see him about anything in particular?" asked Frasquita.

Some new, softer quality in the girl's voice caused Marlene to look at her more closely. There was something different about her expression, too. A certain satisfaction?

Marlene shook her head. "Nothing, really. Only to report progress on the job, but I daresay I shall see him this evening."

"I expect so." Frasquita produced a letter from her pocket. "By the way, Ramon asked me to give you this. He will be coming to the hotel this evening if you wish to see him."

"Thank you."

Marlene went out to her car, and there opened Ramon's letter. It was to ask her to have dinner with him that evening. He would call at the hotel at nine-thirty and hoped her answer would be yes.

"I shall be honoured and delighted," he wrote. "Also you will have the satisfaction of knowing you will be helping two people who are really in love to be together."

Marlene put the letter back into its envelope thoughtfully. Would she really be helping to bring two people together who were in love? Frasquita was, no doubt, but Juan? He gave no indication of his feelings whatever. Marlene imagined he would soon let a woman know if he were in love with her without any outside help.

She set off first for Pineda to look at the plants in the greenhouse and to have a word with Alfonso. It was from Alfonso that she learned Juan had already been to the Hotel del Jardin, looked at the greenhouse and its contents and then left. This news disquieted Marlene a little. Why had he not waited for her and accompanied her here? Was he really so annoyed about last night? But they had talked over the matter of Ramon and his visiting her flat, and Juan had told her to feel free to invite whomever she wished.

She told herself she was worrying about nothing. Juan had finished showing her around. He now expected her simply to get on with her work and to visit which hotels suited her. He had every right to do his rounds in any way he wished.

From the Hotel del Jardin she made her way to the other hotel in Pineda, the Bella Vista, hoping perhaps that Juan might be there, but he was not. Rather than have plants outside the hotel which were looking shabby, Marlene decided to take up those which were there. Empty spaces looked better than plants which no care in the world would revive again.

She decided to have her lunch at the Hotel del Jardin, and when she arrived she found Juan there too, much to her joy and delight. He was sitting at a table in a secluded corner of the dining room. She went over to him, her hand outstretched in a greeting which matched her feelings, hoping his apparent disapproval of the previous evening was forgotten.

He rose from his seat and took her hand, but there was no answering smile on his face.

"Won't you join me?" he said. "I was about to have lunch."

In all politeness he could not say anything else,

Marlene realized, abashed at his cool reception of her.

"I—if you would rather be alone, I—I don't mind sitting somewhere else," she told him.

He gave what sounded like an exasperated sigh. "If I had wanted to be alone, I would not have invited you to join me. Please sit down and tell me how the job has been progressing during my absence. I see you already have the greenhouse in use."

Employer to employee, came the thought as she sat down opposite him. Her joy at having him back was rapidly changing into quite unreasonable hurt feelings. True, he was her employer, but she had thought they were becoming friends, and she had wanted, first, to tell him how glad she was to see him back, and to put right any misunderstanding of last night. If this was the way he had behaved towards Frasquita, first showing friendliness and interest and then withdrawing and becoming the distant employer, no wonder she was unhappy. But then Frasquita was in love with him. She, Marlene, was not.

So Marlene gave him a résumé of her progress with the work and informed him of her plans and ideas for the future programme.

"By April or May, according to the weather, I hope to have a plentiful supply of plants like roses and geraniums in full bloom and ready for planting out."

"Better make it April," he told her. "I think you'll find it warm enough by then. It's the dry month of August you may find difficult."

"I suppose so. But we do have our heatwaves in my country, too. If plants are kept fed and watered they will continue to flower no matter how hot."

He smiled. "I can see that you know your job. But then I knew that before I asked you to come here."

So much for Ramon and his romantic notions of Juan's motive in offering her the job, Marlene thought ruefully.

A waitress brought their first course and conversation flagged for a short while. Glancing around at the other diners in the restaurant, Marlene noticed that a great proportion of them were middle-aged or elderly. She commented on the fact.

Juan nodded. "They're your countrymen—and women. The travel agents offer cheap winter holiday terms especially for pensioners. It's a good idea. It gets them out and away from their surroundings, gives them a winter break, and they enjoy the rest and change. At their age, people don't want to lie on the beach in the sun like the young. Why don't you go along and talk to a few of them after lunch? I'm sure they'll be delighted."

Marlene said she would. She wanted to ask him about his trip, to tell him she had missed him, to explain why Ramon was in her flat last night, but did not seem to find an opening. At last, however, towards the end of their meal, she asked:

"Did you—want to see me about anything special when you came to my flat last night?"

"No, no. I'm sorry I intruded," he said stiffly.

"But, Juan, I'd like to explain to you about that," she began. He cut her short, however.

"No explanations are necessary. I've already told you, you are quite free to have whomsoever you like in your flat. Please say no more about it." He rose. "Now, if you will excuse me, I have to go."

Marlene gazed after him with a sigh. Perhaps she was making too much fuss about a matter he did not deem important. At all events, clearly he did not want to discuss it. She noticed he had made no mention of his three-day trip. Was it because he wanted to keep their relationship on a more businesslike level from now on? She sighed again, and decided to go and talk to some of the English guests, several of whom were now in the lounge having coffee.

As Juan had predicted, the ones with whom she entered into conversation seemed very pleased indeed to talk to someone different, and were most interested in her job here.

"It will be lovely for you in the summer—like being on holiday all the time," one elderly lady said.

"You like it here?" another elderly lady asked.

"Oh, yes. Pineda's a wonderful little place. There are plenty of shops to look at, that lovely square, and you can get to lots of places along the coast."

After a while Marlene got in her car and went along to the two hotels in Lloret and attended to the plants there, returning to Blanes in time for tea, after which, she planned to do some work in the paved garden at the Hotel Marina. On and off she pondered over Ramon's invitation. *Would* it help to leave Juan and Frasquita together? She found it very difficult to decide, difficult, too, to make up her mind whether to accept Ramon's invitation simply for its own sake. One thing she did feel sure of, and that was, she really ought not to let the feud or whatever it was between Juan and Ramon affect her too much. What's the use? Her not seeing Ramon would surely do little to heal the rift. If Juan disliked him so why did he not either forbid him the hotel or ask Frasquita to leave? Could it be that he was a little in love without knowing it? Men were often slow to appreciate what was under their noses. How many private secretaries had been in love with their boss for years before it occurred to him that she was something more than just a piece of office furniture? She supposed love was never very far from the forefront of a woman's mind, whereas a man kept business in the forefront of his. Making a pass at a pretty girl was a far different thing from being in love.

All of which brought her no nearer to making up her mind whether or not to dine with Ramon. Truth to tell she did not particularly want to. She would much prefer to have it downstairs with Juan. Correction—Juan *and Frasquita.*

Juan and Frasquita. Why, she did not know, but the two names repeated themselves over and over in her mind. She went into her kitchenette impatiently. It was silly—there had not been the slightest evidence that Juan remotely cared for the girl. Unless, of course, his inclusion of herself had been designed to—to put Frasquita off or to make her jealous?

Marlene wished she could get their 'problem' out of her mind. It was nothing to do with her. Ramon, too, should mind his own business. All she had to do was to decide whether to accept Ramon's invitation to dinner. If it were merely a matter of leaving Juan and Frasquita together she could doubtless cook up a light meal in her own kitchen, but she was reasonably sure that would cause too much comment, especially if she did it more than once. And once would scarcely be enough to help the cause of love.

For the first time since leaving home Marlene wished she had some friends of her own, someone to talk things over with, someone with whom to spend an evening. She smiled to herself. Brenda would think Ramon terribly romantic. And Molly? Molly would be sensible and advise leaving Juan and Frasquita to work out their own lives.

Marlene was just about to pour water into her teapot when there came a knock on the door. She opened it to see Micaela standing there. She spoke in Spanish, and Marlene found she knew enough to glean that Señor de Montserrat wished her to take tea with him downstairs.

"I'll be down in a few moments," she told the girl.

After a swift look in the mirror Marlene made her way down to Juan's sitting room. Micaela was just bringing in a tray of tea.

"I was just about to make my own upstairs," Marlene told him, taking a seat and wondering whether she had been invited or merely summoned. "Shall I pour?"

"Thank you, yes. You managed to understand Micaela's message? I told her not to try to give it to you in English."

"Yes, I understood."

"You must have been doing some studying while I've been away," he observed.

"Of course." She passed his tea to him.

"Good. Then perhaps we can skip lessons this evening. I thought you might like to go to Rosamar's to see the *flamenco*."

The unexpectedness of the invitation took her aback in view of the things Ramon had talked about, and she scarcely knew what to say except 'Oh'.

Juan watched her expression closely. There seemed no escape from those discerning eyes of his.

"Have you perhaps a previous engagement—with Ramon, for instance?"

She shook her head, too confused to make a split-second decision to accept Ramon's invitation.

"Well then, that's settled."

Settled! She looked at him in astonishment. Had it been any other man she would have reminded him that she had not yet consented.

"Well?" he demanded. "Does the idea not please you?"

"Oh—oh yes, but as it happens I—I was thinking of having dinner in my flat."

"Alone?"

"Why, yes."

"You will do no such thing," he said firmly. "I absolutely forbid it. You will wear your nicest evening clothes and have dinner at Rosamar's, then see the show."

Forbid! At first, anger and indignation rose in her throat. She could not take that from any man. Then suddenly she laughed.

"All right, Juan, you win. Thank you very much. I would love to come."

A slow smile creased his face. "Good," he said in a more gentle tone, then handed her a plate of dainty sandwiches he had made in the kitchen. "Better eat something. You had your lunch early by our standards and it will be a long time before dinner."

Later, as she was dressing for the evening—and not without a great deal of pleasurable anticipation—she wondered rather uneasily what Ramon's reaction would be when he discovered she was going to Rosamar's with Juan. Perhaps she should try to get in touch with him through Frasquita. She wanted to avoid, if possible, a personal confrontation with him. She was reasonably sure that he would be very annoyed, though he had no real right to be. If she could prevent his coming to pick her up she would feel much happier.

Dressed in a long evening skirt and a glittering top, Marlene took her wrap over her arm and went downstairs in search of Frasquita. A light under the door of Juan's room told her he would probably be dressing, so that she would be able to speak to Frasquita alone.

Frasquita was in the office. Her dark eyes opened wide as she saw the way Marlene was dressed.

"You've accepted Ramon's invitation?" she asked, her face aglow with smiles. "He will be pleased—and may I say how charming you look."

114

At this assumption Marlene's heart sank. It was going to be all the more difficult to explain, and she realized she had done the wrong thing entirely by coming to find Frasquita. It would have been better, after all, to have faced Ramon or perhaps have left a note for him.

"Thank you, Frasquita, that's very nice of you, but I—I was wondering whether I could get in touch with Ramon. Could you get his telephone number for me?"

Frasquita's face clouded over again. "But why? He's coming to collect you here, is he not? Why do you want to telephone him?"

Marlene chafed at her inability to think quickly enough. Now there was nothing she could do except tell the other girl the truth.

"I want to tell him I can't accept his invitation. I thought to save him calling for me."

Frasquita's eyes grew wide, but this time with anger. "Then why are you dressed like this? You would not wear such clothes to stay in the hotel, and you would not go out to dinner alone. You do not know any other man in Blanes except—" She grasped Marlene's arm, and her fingers felt like steel. "You are going out somwhere with Juan?"

"Please, Frasquita—" Marlene removed the girl's hand from her arm and rubbed the painful spot left by her grip. "I'm sorry, truly, but he asked me and I couldn't very well refuse."

Frasquita covered her face with her hands. "How could he? How *could* he?" Then with a sudden movement her arms dropped to her sides and she gave Marlene a look of pure dislike. "Why did you come here? I hate you!" she ground out. "I hate you, do you hear?"

Marlene looked at her horrified. She could scarcely believe her ears. She would never have thought

Frasquita capable of such a passionate outburst. She had appeared so quiet and calm, so docile and gentle.

"Frasquita, please—don't talk like that. I—I couldn't help it, really. I—I'm sorry about everything, but—" She paused. It was difficult to know what to say. Useless to say things like: *Everything will turn out all right.* Or: *You and I can still be friends.* She grasped the girl by the shoulders in an effort to show sympathy. But Frasquita brought her fists down on Marlene's arms quite violently.

"Don't touch me! Get out of here! I wish I never had to set eyes on you again!"

Utterly bewildered by this unexpected show of antagonism, Marlene turned to go out of the room, only to see Juan standing there, his face dark.

"What is the meaning of all this?"

Marlene glanced swiftly at the other girl. It would be quite wrong to expect her to give any kind of explanation in her present state. She turned to Juan feeling suddenly quite calm and on top of the situation, at least for the moment.

"I think we ought to go, Juan. Frasquita is far too upset to talk now."

"Very well," he said, after a pause. "I will see you in the morning, Frasquita."

Deeply regretting that she had not left well alone, Marlene went out with Juan. How terribly she had underestimated the depth of Frasquita's feelings for Juan.

Juan glanced at Marlene's face. "May I ask for some explanation from you at the extraordinary scene I witnessed?"

"I—what did you witness?" she asked, trying to think what to say, and what not to say to him. Obviously, she could not tell him the whole truth.

"I heard you apologizing for something and I saw

Frasquita almost break your arms. What was it all about?"

Marlene realized he would have to be told at least part of the truth. The whole truth was not her concern.

"I'm afraid it was to do with Ramon and myself."

From the wheel of his car he glanced at her sharply. "In what way?"

"Well, he—he had asked me to have dinner with him this evening, and she was annoyed because I—I had declined. I was foolish enough to ask how I could get in touch with him to tell him. The—affection between the brother and sister is very strong."

Juan started the car and drove off in the direction of Lloret.

"Acknowledging the undoubtedly strong family ties which exist in Spain, it still seems extraordinary to me that Frasquita should react so violently."

"It was a surprise to me, too. She always seems so quiet and calm."

"Yes," he said thoughtfully. Then he reminded her after a pause: "I *did* ask you if you had a prior engagement this evening."

"I know. He asked me yesterday. I still hadn't made up my mind when you asked me. So—"

"And would you have accepted his invitation if I hadn't asked you?"

"Probably," she answered briefly, and took a covert glance at his expression.

There was the ghost of a smile around his mouth, and she couldn't help wondering the reason for it. Was it that he considered he had scored a point over Ramon? At all events he appeared to find something amusing. The next moment, however, his smile had gone.

"All that is still no excuse for Frasquita's behaviour," she said.

Shocked as she had been by Frasquita's outburst against her, Marlene still felt a certain sympathy for the girl.

"Please let the matter drop, Juan," she pleaded. "I can understand her being angry, and as her anger was directed only against me, I hope you won't say anything to her about what you witnessed. It would only make matters worse."

He was silent for a minute or two, and Marlene fervently hoped that he wouldn't accuse her of arguing again. But he said:

"You're very generous and forgiving. It shall be as you wish. I shall say nothing to her. And now, here we are at Rosamar's. Let us enjoy the evening."

He parked the car on the sea-front quite close to the night-club and they entered the place together. Inside, Marlene experienced a most pleasant surprise at the lushness of the decor. The whole impression was one of colour and comfort. Marlene contrasted this fleetingly with the *bodega* to which Ramon had taken her. But there simply was no comparison.

At the far end of the room was a small stage and dancing area; pink-shaded lamps gave a soft, romantic touch, beaded screens and curtains decorated the walls and divided off alcoves, but the most luxurious touch of all were the chair and settee coverings in rich, burgundy plush velvet. Marlene had never seen anything like it.

As they were shown to their table an orchestra played and several couples were already dancing.

"It pleases you?" asked Juan as her glance ranged around the room once more.

"It's beautiful. Are all your night-clubs like this?"

"They tend to be colourful, yes. It fits the mood of the *flamenco* and of the Spanish people."

They sat for a while and drank a sparkling wine which, Juan told her, the tourists called champagne. But Marlene did not greatly care what it was called. She loved it. Presently Juan asked her to dance, and she found the experience a very, very pleasant one indeed. How easy it would be to fall in love with him, she thought, and suddenly felt the need to steel herself against such a possibility. She had been devastated once by love. She did not want the same thing to happen again.

After they had danced, a menu was brought to them. Marlene left the choice to Juan, and each course which came was more delicious than the last. For hors d'oeuvres they had *jamóns serrano* or mountain ham, which Juan told her was laid out in the sun on the snow of the mountains for the sun to cure it. The snow prevented it from becoming spoilt first. This no doubt accounted for its dark red colour. It was sliced thin and almost translucent.

"Often, we have with it *lomo embuchado*, a long strip of pork cured with paprika and garlic," Juan told her. "But such high seasoning might not agree with you if you're unaccustomed to it as most English people are. In the summer it is delicious served with ice-cold melon."

"It's delicious as it is," she assured him.

It still seemed odd to her that the vegetables and meat were served separately, but the dish called *paella* was very succulent indeed. It was chicken served with saffron-flavoured rice and titbits of seafood—prawns, flakes of fish, small clams and tender pieces of calamares.

Between the courses they danced, and then, just as they had reached the dessert course, a large dais was slid out on top of the dancing area and the show began. At first there was folk-singing and a pair of comedians.

These were followed by a magician who both mystified and astonished the audience. Then finally, the *flamenco* dancers. Their entrance was heralded by the playing of several guitars strummed with tremendous verve and passion which at once transferred itself to the audience so that the whole atmosphere became tense.

Marlene almost gasped aloud as the dancers erupted on to the stage. On occasions at home she had seen what purported to be Spanish dancers, but never had she seen any dressed so magnificently. She had expected the dark-haired girls in their tight bodices and the layers of flounces, but these dresses had at least two yards of flounce which swept the stage. They were in vivid green and black, black and yellow, black and orange, black and turquoise—red. It was difficult to say which was the more attractive. For a moment they stood poised, slim figures firm and taut, their glossy dark hair crowned with mantillas and most impressive of all the traditional proud and haughty look which Marlene felt was much more than simply a superficial expression put on for the purpose of show business.

Arms held high in the characteristic pose, castanets in each palm, the girls began their dance, slow at first, keeping time with the rhythmic strumming of the guitars, full and throaty. There were six dancers altogether. Sometimes they danced in pairs, sometimes four of them, changing places with ease, and those who were not dancing clapping in time with the music. The play of the castanets became faster and faster until the sound was like a continuous purring.

Then they were joined by the male dancer whose arched back and taut muscles told of years of discipline. There was some play between him and the main woman dancer, an exchange of passionate glances, sinuous movements of hands, fingers, wrists and stamping of feet, all of which seemed to be telling a story. Marlene wondered what it was, but dared not break the spell by asking, and soon she was aware of absolutely nothing except the sound of the music, the purring of the castanets and the rhythmic stamping of feet. Marlene felt a strange stirring within her, as if she were at one with the passion of the drama being played out on the stage. Just as the dance appeared to have finished it would start up again with loud cries and a renewal of vigour and passion which was simply staggering.

When at last the company were bowing to the thunderous applause and cheers, Marlene felt almost as breathless as though she had been dancing herself.

"Weren't they terrific?" she said to Juan as she applauded madly with the rest.

Juan nodded. "Yes, they really do perform it well here. And it gets you every time, almost like the beating of the tom-toms gets the Africans."

Marlene thought that a very good analogy. "What's the story of the *flamenco*?" she asked. "I'm sure there is one."

"It's rather obscure. I have heard it said that it depicts a time when there was a great swarm of locusts which threatened to devour all the crops of the land and so bring about starvation to the people. The stamping is to stamp out the locusts, and not until every last one had been killed would the women stop to dally with their men. But that is only hearsay, not the official story. I don't even know whether there is one."

"The 'hearsay' story sounds very possible," said Marlene, her mind picturing again the rhythmic gestures of the dance. "Very, very possible indeed."

Now, the stage had been glided smoothly back into

its original place and dancing was once more in progress. Marlene gave a happy sigh as she watched the couples on the dancing area. She turned to thank Juan for bringing her and saw an inscrutable expression on his face as he looked across the room. Marlene followed his gaze and to her surprise saw Ramon there, and with him was Frasquita.

"Did they know we were coming here?" Marlene asked him.

"I certainly did not tell them."

"Then they must have guessed. Or maybe it's merely a coincidence their being here."

"Nothing Ramon does is ever coincidental," Juan answered in a steely voice. "Everything he does is planned."

"But why? I mean, does it really matter that they're here?" she queried.

"It is almost bound to," he answered. "However, let's dance, shall we?"

It struck Marlene that the brother and sister might not even know that Juan and herself were at the night-club. Perhaps Ramon had suggested it in an effort to cheer his sister up a little. The thought of Frasquita's distress earlier struck Marlene afresh, and a great sympathy for the girl came over her. She *would* try to help her, she decided suddenly. Juan meant so much to her, whereas she, Marlene, scarcely knew him. She was certainly not in love with him.

Juan had risen to escort her on to the dance floor, but Marlene remained in her seat.

"Juan," she said, looking up at him, "as I said something to Frasquita earlier on which upset her, will you help me to make amends by asking her to dance with you?"

He gave her a look of mild surprise. "And how will that help you, may I ask?"

Marlene smiled. "Well, I think she would rather dance with you than with her brother."

"I see," he said distantly. "Very well, if that is what you want. Excuse me, *señorita*."

Marlene watched him cross the room, aware that she had annoyed him. He was a man who liked to make his own decisions.

As she expected, as Juan led Frasquita on to the dance floor, Ramon crossed the room to herself.

"Good evening, *señorita*. So we meet this evening, after all. May I sit down?"

"Do. Tell me, Ramon, did you guess we might be here?"

His shoulders lifted, and she thought at first that he was not going to answer her question. But he said abruptly, "Yes, I did."

"And did Frasquita know there was a chance of finding Juan here with me?"

Ramon's dark eyes held hers broodingly. "She was very, very angry and upset."

Marlene sighed. "I know. And I'm sorry."

"How could you do this to my sister? Surely Juan means nothing to you?"

"I wouldn't say that exactly," she told him quietly. "I have a great respect for Juan both as my employer and as a man. In view of your sister's upset this evening, however, I *will* help her all I can."

CHAPTER SEVEN

AS soon as she had spoken the words Marlene felt a
vague sense of uneasiness. It was not that she was
already regretting her decision to try to help Frasquita
to win Juan's love. It was something on which she
could not quite put her finger. Unless—

"It will have to be done very discreetly," she told
Ramon. "If he suspects for a moment that we're
scheming to manoeuvre him in any way he is likely
to be extremely angry, with the opposite result to the
one you wish to achieve."

Gone was Ramon's brooding expression. His eyes
were bright and his face wreathed in smiles.

"There is only one way to do it. You must pretend
to be in love with me. And who knows—"

But Marlene shook her head. "I'm pretending
nothing of the kind."

"But if you do not have a beau he will think you
are free to accept any invitation he offers."

"I *shall* be free. Free to decline."

"Will you come out with me when I ask you?"

"Sometimes, yes."

"Good. Let you and me dance also."

Hoping she was doing the right thing and had not
spoilt Juan's evening by splitting up their twosome
Marlene danced with Ramon, searching the throng
for a sight of Juan and Frasquita. The floor was
crowded now, and some of the couples doing very
little but swaying in time to the dreamy music in each
other's arms. Aware that Ramon was holding her too
closely for comfort she at last found Juan and

Frasquita. They, too, were dancing close together, Frasquita's arm almost around Juan's neck. It would seem that Frasquita had decided to change her attitude from that of a passive, heartbroken and rejected woman to one who was now determined to fight for her love. And what about Juan? Would he welcome her attention? Marlene tried to get a better look at him now, but he had already become lost again in the crowd.

When the music stopped Ramon suggested that they should leave Frasquita and Juan alone together, and that Marlene and himself should go and get a drink at the long bar.

But Marlene shook her head at this. "I can't do that—it wouldn't be right. Juan brought me here. I'm his guest."

Ramon gave that characteristic shrug of his shoulders, and with barely good grace led her back to the table at which she had been sitting with Juan.

Juan was already there, and with him Frasquita. "Won't you join us?" he said to Ramon, and signalled a waiter to bring two more chairs.

"Well, and did you enjoy the *flamenco*, Marlene?" Ramon asked, giving her his full attention.

"Of course. It was wonderful." Embarrassed by the way Ramon was looking at her, Marlene turned to speak to Frasquita. "What a happy coincidence that you, too, decided to come here this evening."

Frasquita eyed her coolly. "As this is the best night-club for miles around outside of Barcelona it's not so surprising. And of course, Juan and I have been here many times, have we not, Juan?"

She turned a devastating smile full upon him. His own face relaxed into a smile.

"Indeed we have, Frasquita. Indeed we have."

Ramon put his hand on Marlene's arm. "Come on,

Marlene, let's dance again."

A new number had only just started. He was certainly not giving Juan a chance to ask her. Marlene turned to him.

"Do you mind, Juan?"

He gave a gesture which said, *why ask me?* "Go ahead. Frasquita and I will probably sit this one out."

"There you are," Ramon said as they reached the dance floor. "I've told Frasquita over and over again : 'either find another job or go all out to get him'."

"I thought you considered that kind of thing undignified for your sister?"

He shrugged. "Not if it is done cleverly. You women know how to do these things. Tonight she was so angry when she learned that it was Juan who was taking you out and not I she put on her battledress, so to speak. So with a little help also from you and from me—"

"All right, Ramon, let's leave it at that, shall we? I shall do my best to avoid Juan and decline invitations out whenever possible. But as he's my employer, it may not always be easy. Remember that."

She felt distinctly uneasy and couldn't help wishing she could have avoided becoming involved in the private lives of such a tempestuous people. But she reflected wryly that in this life it was almost impossible *not* to get involved in the private lives of those whom one met every day and worked alongside.

The evening had lost its enchantment. It was not until past midnight that Juan said to her :

"Well, Marlene, are you going to have another dance with me before we go?"

She gave him a startled look. She wanted to dance with him, but felt embarrassed because of what she was doing. Then she felt a gentle kick from Ramon under the table. A hint that she should decline, if she wanted to help Frasquita.

So all in all, she shook her head. "Will you excuse me, Juan? I'm feeling rather tired."

Ramon was quick to seize the advantage. "In that case I'll run you home. I've got my car outside. Juan will bring Frasquita home, I've no doubt."

"Naturally," answered Juan. "Although," he added suddenly, "I think it would be wisest if I return Frasquita to the hotel and you take her home from there. Meanwhile, she and I will have a last dance."

He said goodnight to Marlene and held out his hand to Frasquita. Not feeling too happy, Marlene allowed Ramon to lead her to the exit. If only Ramon had not come to Rosamar's, she thought suddenly. She would much preferred to have finished the evening happily with Juan. She hated this conspiracy, even if it was in a desire to help.

"Why did Juan think it wiser for you to run Frasquita home from the hotel?" she asked as she slid into the passenger seat of Ramon's car.

Ramon grunted. "He is afraid that if he took her home his intentions would be taken seriously. I have a good mind to drop you at the hotel and then go home quickly."

"No, Ramon! You mustn't do that. You must not force Juan's hand. I'm sure your sister would not wish it, either. Let things happen naturally. Juan will show his intentions when he is ready."

She thought these strict conventions of the Spanish people made life very complicated. How much more simple life was, in comparison, in her own country.

Juan and Frasquita were a mere five minutes after Ramon and Marlene in arriving back at the hotel. To make sure that Ramon did wait for his sister Marlene stayed in the foyer and talked to him until Juan and Frasquita put in an appearance.

Marlene had intended to go straight upstairs, but somehow she wanted to linger, to talk to Juan, to find out how he had really felt about Ramon turning up at the night-club as he had with Frasquita, to make sure he was not angry with herself, and that all was well between them.

Juan saw Frasquita to the door, then turned and stood there for a moment looking in Marlene's direction. As there were few lights now in the foyer she could not see his expression very clearly. She started towards him, feeling she must speak to him, but at that moment the night porter appeared and approached him. She walked slowly towards the lift, unable to understand why she was dithering about so much, or why she felt so miserable.

She made her way to her flat. She had not even had the chance to say good night to him. Was he deliberately avoiding her? she wondered. She took a deep breath and told herself to stop imagining things. She left her door open and kept a listening ear for the sound of him coming up. It was only good manners, she decided, to thank him for the evening. She went into the kitchen to put the kettle on to make a drink, and in about ten minutes she heard the lift door open and close again.

She fled into the corridor. "Juan—"

He paused in the act of inserting his key in the door of his room.

"Yes, Marlene?"

She took a few steps towards him. "I—I want to thank you for taking me tonight. It—it was wonderful."

"What was so wonderful exactly?" he queried without smiling.

"Why, the meal, the show—everything, especially the *flamenco*."

"And the dashing Ramon? I expect he made it all quite perfect. Well, good night, Marlene."

"Good night."

But he was in his room and the door closed almost before she could get the words out. She went slowly back into her flat feeling not one whit happier for her few words with him. The evening *had* been perfect before Ramon had arrived on the scene. He had made an inspired guess, doubtless remembering her telling him that Juan had asked her to Rosamar's at some time. But how much of Ramon's concern was for his sister and how much a private vendetta against Juan?

She undressed for bed and tried to put the whole matter out of her mind. She would dissociate herself from all this intrigue. Maybe after this one visit to show her the *flamenco* he would not ask her out for the evening again. He was merely doing a duty towards a stranger in a foreign country. After this evening he might well become more aware of Frasquita in a personal way. If so, and she fervently hoped this would be the case, then a great many problems would be solved. Juan and Ramon might even temper their dislike of each other. Right relationships were all-important in this world, not only for the individuals concerned, but for those around them.

For the next few days Marlene scarcely saw Juan except for her Spanish lessons, and these he conducted in the most businesslike manner possible. Sensing a change in his attitude towards her, she ventured a suggestion which had been in her mind for quite a number of days.

"Juan, do you think we might reduce the number of Spanish lessons to, say, one a week now? I'm learning quite well on my own. I listen to radio and television whenever possible and—and thought of going to the cinema, too."

Too late, she realized the suggestion should have come from Juan himself. He liked to be the one to change or rearrange things. His face became dark and his lips compressed into a thin line.

"As you wish," he said, after a moment or two. "You are certainly making good progress. You will not, I take it, be going to the cinema alone?"

She had not thought about it. She supposed it was not done in this country—a young lady going unescorted to the cinema. One did not do so from choice at home, but if one wished one could slip into a matinée without comment or fear of breaking some convention.

"No, no," she answered swiftly. "I shall not be going alone."

She knew he would get the impression that Ramon was taking her, but that could not be helped. She had wanted to avoid the kind of reply which might sound like a hint to Juan to take her. She would go with Ramon if he asked her. If not she simply would not go to the cinema. She would watch and listen to whatever was on television.

Juan suggested a day in mid-week for her Spanish lesson, then he said, "I shall be dining out this evening, with some English friends. If they invited you to their house some time, would you go, or is your time from now on going to be fully occupied with Ramon?"

She ignored the latter part of his question and said she would be delighted to meet some English people. She felt she could hardly refuse, though she anticipated that Ramon and Frasquita would not be very pleased.

In the absence of Juan that evening Ramon had dinner with Marlene and Frasquita at the hotel. Frasquita seemed quite a good deal happier than of late, though she did not talk much about Juan. It was

Ramon who later, when Frasquita was out of the room, said there had been a marked difference in his attitude towards her.

"I think at last he is seeing the true worth of my sister, and she is happy. Myself, I do not think he is worthy of her and if he wins her he will be the lucky one, but if she is happy—"

"Have you ever met Juan's English friends?" she asked him.

Ramon's dark brows came together. "You mean the man who hires out yachts to tourists in the summer and his wife who paints pretty pictures?"

"I don't know what they do. Juan hasn't told me. I only know that he wants me to meet them."

"Oh, he does? When?"

But that Marlene could not tell him either.

"And will you go?"

"How could I refuse? Frasquita will have to comfort herself by the fact that we shall not be alone together."

Ramon grunted. "I fear the visit—if it does not include Frasquita—will be one more thorn in her side."

Marlene gave a little sigh. She was beginning to feel not a little impatient with all this concentration on Frasquita's feelings.

"Being in love is quite a common complaint, Ramon. Your sister will have to be patient and not expect everything to go the way she would like all at once. Has she never had a boy-friend or been in love before?" she asked with sudden curiosity.

Ramon slowly shook his head. "She may have been, but we in Spain are not so promiscuous as in some other countries. Too many *novios* can soon give a girl a bad reputation. Their courting is done in public. Kissing and holding hands is frowned upon."

131

"But how on earth can they get to know each other properly if they are never alone together to talk to each other?"

"They can talk without being alone and in secret. It is not right for a boy and girl who are in love to be alone together. It is better they are together in the company of their friends."

Marlene did not argue further. Perhaps it was right for Spain. Who was she to judge? She had certainly noticed, on the days when she went for a walk along the bay, or what was known as a *maestranza*, that groups of girls and groups of boys would wander in opposite directions. Frasquita, of course, was not still a girl. She was a woman. With so many restrictions put upon young men and women meeting, Marlene reflected that it was a wonder that half the population were not bachelors and spinsters.

Marlene began to notice herself, in the weeks that followed, that Juan was more gentle in his behaviour towards Frasquita, though convention, it seemed, prevented his taking her out for an evening unless she were accompanied by her brother or they formed a party with others.

Marlene was beginning to think that Juan's friends did not wish to meet her, or that Juan had forgotten about the matter, but one day about the middle of March she received a note signed Jane Saunders, inviting her to lunch on the following Sunday.

If you can make it, just let Juan know. He'll be bringing you, in any case, the note finished.

"Are you free?" Juan asked her when she mentioned the note to him. "Not seeing Ramon?"

Marlene wished he wouldn't keep taking it for granted that she saw Ramon so often and so regularly, but supposed it all helped what might be termed the course of true love. If he thought she was preoccupied with Ramon he was less likely to think she needed taking around by himself. She said she was free that particular Sunday, and Juan arranged to set off for the house of his friends at eleven o'clock.

"Is it far?" she asked.

"No, no. About twenty miles inland, that's all."

The weather was chilly and inclined to rain. Marlene thought a trouser suit would be in order and wore one in a bright yellow with a white sweater. Frasquita was on duty, and Marlene caught a dark, brooding expression on the girl's face as she followed Juan out to his car. Marlene hesitated for a fraction. Should she pause and have a word with her—reassure her? She decided not to. For one thing there might be another scene. A jealous woman is not one to be reasoned with. And for another thing, Frasquita would have to learn to take these disappointments, to be patient. From all accounts of the Spanish way of life mistrust and jealousy after marriage would avail a woman nothing. And she and Juan were quite some way off marriage yet.

Juan drove the car up the Avenida José Antonio out of the town in a north-easterly direction. After they had left the main roads the going became very bumpy indeed, with some of the minor roads little more than cart tracks. She hung on the safety strap and asked, laughing, if there were many roads like this in Spain.

"Quite a number," Juan told her. "Roads cost money, so we have tended to concentrate on the main roads only. The Spaniard does not like to be taxed too heavily, and not quite every man has a car as they apparently do in some other countries. Economic growth in Spain has been slow. We've been pretty isolated from the rest of the world in both financial and business practices. We are neither communist nor capitalist, and economics have remained somewhat subservient to politics. But I mustn't bore you with our politics."

"Oh, you're not boring me," she assured him. "I'm most interested. Please go on."

"Well, briefly, a group of planners who had grown up since the Civil War persuaded Franco to join a body called the Organization for Economic Co-operation which achieved something like a miracle in Spanish industry. No miracle, however, has yet touched Spanish agriculture. It's a beautiful country, but our dramatic, rocky land is not very well suited to farming."

"Some miracles take a little longer," said Marlene.

He gave her a swift glance. "That's a very profound observation. You're probably right. Plans *are* afoot for our agriculture—land irrigation and scientific farming. But progress is slow, whereas in industry rapid strides have been made. Our factories are turning out gas stoves, washing machines and refrigerators and—a new idea for us—hire-purchase is getting the goods into the homes of the people."

The journey to the house of Juan's friends was all too short for Marlene. She loved hearing Juan talk and was tremendously interested in all he had to tell her about his country. Ramon never talked about any of these things.

"How long have your friends lived in Spain?" she asked as they entered the little village at the foot of a range of mountains.

"About five years, I think. I've known them for nearly four. Paul does a tourist trade in yacht hire on the beach in the summer and he sometimes used to drop into the hotel. We got chatting one day and he invited me to meet his wife."

He drew up outside a long, low house built of stone, wood and clay.

"It was several small cottages when Jane and Paul first bought it," Juan explained. "And near derelict. They cleaned it up, repaired it and made it into one."

"Who did they belong to originally?"

"Some poor farmers. They left them for the city factory as many have done. The life of the small farmer is very hard."

At the sound of the car the young couple came out to greet them. Paul was bronzed and dark-haired and wore a pair of slacks and a sweater. Jane was fair and slightly built with a bright welcoming smile, and she, too, wore slacks and a sweater.

"Hello, there!" Paul called out.

Juan made the introductions and all shook hands before moving towards the door of the house.

"How do you like it?" Jane asked Marlene, whose interest was held by the unusual construction of the building.

"It's fascinating. Juan tells me it was nearly derelict when you bought it."

Jane laughed. "But it was cheap—and that was the main thing. It leaked—at least, the roof did. There were few windows and what there were had no glass in them. It was a little tempting to render the whole thing over and paint it white, but in the end we decided to restore it with the same materials it had been built with originally."

Inside the house the decor and furnishings were simple. The rough walls were painted white, which made a perfect background for the many pictures painted by Jane.

"We've got so many we can ring the changes any time we become bored with any of them," she said brightly. "And I've got stacks of small ones in readiness for the coming season. The tourists like to buy them as presents. I've painted the bay at Blanes so

135

many times I could do it in my sleep."

"You don't get bored by painting the same thing over and over again?" Marlene asked her.

"Not really. I'm not a great artist. I know my limitations, and if I find I'm getting bored with the bay I do something else. Like this *flamenco* dancer, for instance."

She pointed to a large canvas, and great artist or not, Marlene thought it was very good. So were they all.

"I'd like to buy one like that," she said as she stood before the picture of the dancer so like those she had seen at the night-club. "You've got the folds of the dress, the flounces, the figure of the dancer and the haughty look on her face exactly right."

Jane laughed. "Why, thank you. Here—" she lifted the picture from the wall, "have this as a present from me."

"Oh, but I couldn't!" protested Marlene. "You must let me pay for it."

"No, no. Do have it, please. I've got several more like it." Jane turned to Juan. "Take it out to the car to make sure she has it."

"Thank you very much. It's very kind of you," Marlene smiled, wishing she had thought to bring Jane a plant of some kind.

"What made you decide to live in Spain?" Marlene asked as they drank a glass of sherry before the meal.

"We just fell in love with Blanes, I suppose," answered Paul.

"Not to mention the climate," added Jane. "We came here so often we suddenly thought: 'Why not come here to live?' Paul was keen on sailing and hated the idea of a nine-to-five job. So we looked around for somewhere to live. Properties in Blanes were far too high for us—and one day when we were touring around we found these three cottages."

"And heigh-ho, it was us for the simple life," Paul added. "Unlike Juan here, who lives in hotel splendour."

Juan smiled. "I'm thinking of finding a house for myself. Or having one built. Living in a hotel has its drawbacks—has it not, Marlene?"

Marlene was rather taken aback at this sudden directing of conversation into personal channels, and scarcely knew how to answer it. She decided to be evasive.

"It can be convenient," she answered. "But I wouldn't care to live in a hotel—no matter how com-fortable and convenient—for the rest of my life."

"You mean, not if you were married," Jane said.

"Well, yes, I suppose so. I should think when you're married you need to be completely alone to—to work things out, not be surrounded by other people."

"But, Marlene," put in Juan soberly, "surely there will always be other people around. A married couple cannot isolate themselves altogether."

"Marlene has a point," Paul said before Marlene could reply to Juan. "You need to be able to shout at each other, to throw things at each other even, without neighbours or relatives putting their oar in."

"Is that what you were thinking of?" Juan asked her.

"Not quite. I should hope—er—for my part—that my husband and I could adjust to married life without resort to shouting or throwing things. But in Juan's case, for instance," she went on, thinking of Frasquita and himself living at the Hotel Marina, "there would always be someone—a member of the staff or a guest —intruding with requests, something or someone demanding their attention."

"When they might be in the middle of talking out a

137

quarrel or misunderstanding?" added Jane.

"Something like that." Then she laughed and asked jokingly: "Did you and Paul shout and throw things when you were first married?"

Jane shook her head. "Not quite, but we had our arguments and period of adjustment, didn't we, Paul?"

"Of course. I imagine all couples do. But circumstances vary. People in show business, for instance. They can't usually be in the same place together for very long, still less alone together."

"Perhaps that's why the divorce rate among them is so high," Jane said.

"And that's why Juan wants a house," answered Paul promptly.

Jane's blue eyes widened. "Are you thinking of getting married, Juan? Or are we being a little premature—not to mention tactless?"

Marlene was somewhat staggered at this turn in the conversation. Obviously, Juan had been saying something to Paul about wanting a house. Had things progressed as far as that between Frasquita and himself? She tried to read his face, but his expression was impassive.

"What man isn't thinking of getting married?" he answered easily. "But you're premature in that I haven't asked the lady yet," he told Jane. "I want to be sure the answer is going to be yes."

Marlene would have thought Frasquita's answer could be guaranteed, but perhaps when actually alone in his company she was more reserved, and did not quite wear her heart on her sleeve.

During lunch Marlene learned that Paul actually built his own sailing dinghies, using a basic hull and fibreglass. These he constructed in a workshop at the back of the house.

While Jane and Marlene did the washing up Juan went out with Paul to have a look at the latest one being built.

"How are you liking Spain?" Jane asked Marlene as they washed and dried the dishes. "Do you think you're going to be happy and settle here?"

Marlene hesitated. They were not easy questions to answer, and she was never the one to make polite replies instead of telling the truth.

"I like the country, at least, what I've seen of it so far, and the people. But whether I shall settle down for good or not it's too soon to say."

"What's the trouble? Frasquita?" Jane asked shrewdly.

"In a way, yes."

Jane smiled. "I thought she might be. She'e very jealous and possessive of Juan. Always has been since we've known him. He was telling us how he met you and asked you to come back with him. I hope you don't mind."

"Not in the least." Marlene thought for a moment, then as she remembered her belongings left behind in store she said: "I think I shall probably have to make up my mind in another month or so." She told Jane something of her past life and about her father's antique furniture. "I can't leave them there indefinitely."

Jane hung up the tea towels to dry. "They'd come in very useful if you married and settled down here."

Marlene laughed shortly. "I don't think I'm likely to marry a native of this country—from all I hear of the status of women and her place in society."

"I know what you mean. But suppose you fell in love with one of them? What then?"

"Heaven forbid! I've heard Ramon's ideas on the subject of women."

"And Juan's?"

"Juan is perhaps a little more liberal in his ideas, but—" She shook her head. He would in all probability marry Frasquita, in any case.

"You might, of course, meet an Englishman living in this country. What then?" queried Jane.

Marlene laughed. "You're very anxious to see me married, aren't you? I don't think I want to, myself, yet. I've had one unhappy experience. I don't want another for a long time." Then, to change the subject, "Juan has given me a very nice flat. Why don't you come over and see me some time?"

Jane said she would like to, then suddenly: "You mentioned Frasquita's brother Ramon just now. Do you see much of him?"

"He comes to the hotel a good deal," Marlene fenced.

"But you haven't been out with him?"

"Once or twice, yes, but—" She broke off worriedly.

Jane eyed her keenly. "But what? You can tell me anything you like. I'm as close as an oyster if need be."

"It's—a sort of feud between Juan and Ramon. It makes me uneasy."

"It's easily explained, and it's really no secret among those who know them, though they probably don't talk about it themselves. They were once in love with the same woman."

Marlene frowned. "But what happened? Neither appears to have won."

"Juan was winning all right, but Ramon got up to all kinds of tricks. She broke off with Juan and ended up by marrying a bullfighter. But they've never forgiven each other."

It was all clear now. Perhaps, having once loved so deeply, Juan would, like herself, be slow to love again. And with all this between himself and Ramon it was surprising that his sister still worked for Juan. Marlene was about to ask Jane if she had any knowledge of friends of Juan's in what Ramon had termed his 'mountain retreat', but Juan and Paul came back into the room and so the topic of conversation came to an end.

Paul asked Marlene if she would be interested in seeing his boat and she said she would, so they went out to the workshop together leaving Juan and Jane behind. Marlene did find it interesting.

"I think you're very clever," she told him as he pointed out to her his method of layer after layer of glass fibre on to his basic model, the same one that he used for all his boats.

He laughed. "There's nothing to it, really, but I'm crazy about boats. I understand you're something of a wizard yourself—with plants."

"I wouldn't say that. Like you, I'm just crazy about anything that grows—even weeds in the right place. Did you know, for instance, that butterflies are attracted to nettles?"

"No, I didn't. But that's life, isn't it? You get the nicest people—perhaps some decorative woman—simply mad about some boor of a man."

Marlene laughed. "I've never looked at it that way before. It only goes to prove that there's something attractive about everybody, no matter how *un*attractive they may appear to the majority."

Paul put his hand on her shoulder. "I think it was a lucky day for Spain when you arrived. I hope you'll stay. Juan is not the only one who finds you an asset. Jane needs someone like you, too."

She looked at him in puzzled surprise, but he laughed at her expression and gave her a gentle push.

"Let's get back to the others."

It was four o'clock when Juan announced that they must be getting back to the hotel, and with smiles and waves and 'see you again soon' Juan drove away.

"Nice couple," Marlene said as they left the village.

"They've certainly taken a strong liking to you," he answered in an odd tone of voice.

"Shouldn't they have?" she queried.

He was silent for a moment, then he asked: "What makes you say a thing like that?"

Marlene silently fumed against herself for her tactlessness. She could hardly say it had been because of something in his voice. That would be courting an argument.

"I'm sorry. It was a silly thing to say. It's just that—" she added on a sudden thought, "they're your friends. I wouldn't want to intrude on that."

"You worry too much," he told her. "Now that you've met them you can see them any time you like—and they like. You don't have to wait for me or include me. That was the whole object of taking you to meet them. The village is fairly easy to find. But I'll write out some directions for you."

Marlene thanked him and they fell silent. It seemed to her that he was trying to tell her not to expect a foursome each time she saw Jane and Paul. Was this to appease Frasquita or to make sure that Jane and Paul did not get the wrong idea about her own relationship with him? Another thought occurred to her, too. Was he perhaps making sure that she herself did not get any wrong ideas?

All these thoughts saddened her. She almost began to wish she had not come here. She had run away from one unhappy situation only to become involved in another. She determined, in future, to stop worrying about them all—Juan, Frasquita, Ramon—and just attend to her job. She could hardly leave now when spring was just around the corner. Soon she would be setting out plants. Already she had had to lower the heating in her greenhouse and open the door and windows for longer periods. But towards the end of the summer, then perhaps she would think about going back home again.

Telling herself to stop worrying, however, about these three people in whose lives she had become involved did not stop her from thinking a good deal about them, and in particular about Juan. Another week went by and she realized that, by and large, he was scarcely out of her mind. As she went from one of the hotels to another looking after the plants she found she was constantly watching out for him, hoping to see him. Each time she saw him talking to Frasquita she felt what she could only describe as a twinge of jealousy. She did not like this in the least. She was not given to petty jealousy, and could not figure it out. Then one day she was about to enter the office when she saw Juan in there with Frasquita, his arm across her shoulders.

Marlene turned abruptly and made her way upstairs to her flat and tried to come to terms with something that was more, much more, than mere jealousy even. She had an agonizingly strong desire to burst into tears. She sat down on the divan and covered her face with her hands. What was the matter with her? Why should she feel like this? It was ridiculous. She must pull herself together. What did it matter to her that Juan was becoming more affectionate towards Frasquita?

She paced around the flat fighting against emotions which crowded in on her. But it was no use. The very last thing she had wanted to happen had done so. She had to face it.

She had fallen in love with Juan de Montserrat.

CHAPTER EIGHT

THE knowledge afforded Marlene no pleasure or satisfaction whatever. On the contrary, it filled her with the utmost dismay and consternation. If he was not actually in love with Frasquita, he was well on the way to being so, judging what she had just witnessed—and she herself had been partly instrumental in bringing it about. And in addition to what she had just seen in the office he was thinking of buying a house.

Marlene sighed and began her restless pacing again. She should have been forewarned when she found herself admiring him and enjoying his company so much. Now, she would have to keep a careful watch on herself in his presence, fight against her feelings for him, as nothing could possibly come of it. It was ironical that she had declared to Jane that she would never marry a native of this country. She had not then reckoned on falling in love with one of them—still less with Juan.

She forced herself to go downstairs again. She had some work to do in the paved garden. To hold the climbing plants she had planned to grow up the walls she had received Juan's permission to have large, decorative stone troughs, and these required to be filled with the right growing medium in order to ensure the plants' uninterrupted growth. She could at least do one thing for Juan—make his gardens and his hotels look as beautiful as she could.

Marlene kept herself as busy as possible in the days which followed, but this did not prevent her from thinking of Juan. He was hardly ever out of her mind, and to make matters worse she pictured him constantly with Frasquita. Frasquita, as dark as she herself was fair. A girl of his own country. She waited each day for the announcement of their engagement, yet dreaded the day when she should know of it.

She saw more of Ramon in the evenings in the hope that in his company she would have less time to think of Juan. He, at any rate, seemed happy at the turn of events.

"She owes much of it to you," he told her. "And we are both very grateful."

"Has he been to see Frasquita's parents yet?" she asked.

Ramon shook his head. "But he will quite soon. One cannot hurry these things. I understand Juan is looking for a house. He will want to be able to tell our parents that he has somewhere suitable in view to begin their married life. Is that the way a man does things in your country?"

"Not usually," Marlene answered unhappily. "A man pops the question first and then starts thinking of where they're going to live. Sometimes he doesn't even pop the question. The pair fall in love and take the rest for granted."

"And what about your permissive society, your 'swinging London'?" asked Ramon.

"It's my belief that's only for the minority, those who imagine they are above the existing social laws. A lot of it is top show only. The majority of us live ordinary decent lives—falling in love perhaps a little younger than our parents did, engaged in the day-to-day business of earning a living and trying to make a home for ourselves and our children."

"That doesn't sound very exciting."

"Life often isn't very exciting, is it?"

"It can be made so. You found the *flamenco* exciting, and it is. Would you like to go again?"

But Marlene shook her head. It would remind her too much of Juan.

But Ramon was not to be deterred. "Then what about having dinner with me in Barcelona—and a tour of the city lights? Now there's an experience for you."

So Marlene agreed. Anything would be better than sitting in her flat the whole evening, and she would also be saved having to dine with Juan and Frasquita, something she was finding more and more of an ordeal. It was not that there was any great display of open affection between them, at least, not on the part of Juan, but there was a distinctly uncomfortable atmosphere which Marlene attributed to her own unhappy state of mind.

She told Juan, as she usually did out of courtesy, that she would be dining out that night.

"I see. With Ramon, I suppose?"

"Yes." Then she went on, on impulse : "Juan, I'm sorry, I know you don't like him very much. I wonder —would you rather I found somewhere else to live? It's hardly fair, anyway, that I should be depriving you of your own flat all this time."

"You're not depriving me of anything," he told her in a flinty voice. "As to my not liking Ramon, the way *you* feel about him is more to the point. You seem to be seeing a great deal of him. I only hope you know what you're doing and that he doesn't let you down."

"I don't see how he can do that," she answered, his tone of voice like a whiplash around her heart.

Life, she decided, was becoming unbearable here. Just as soon as she could she would go back to England. Why had she to go and fall in love all over again? And this time with a depth she had certainly not had for Roger.

The evening in Barcelona with Ramon would have been, as he had said, quite an exciting one in different circumstances. Ramon chose, after all, a night-club where there was *flamenco* dancing, for which she was not in the mood. The *flamenco*, wherever it was performed, would always be associated with Juan, and as she listened once again to its intense, passionate rhythm the ache in her heart was almost intolerable. She was glad to get out into the less personal, but brilliantly lit city. Ramon took her to see the illuminated fountains of Montjuich, a simply breathtaking sight, and then on around the sparkling and floodlit city. It should have been romantic and exciting, and though she appreciated Ramon's taking her she knew that no experience, no matter how unique or thrilling, would be the same without Juan.

It was very late when Ramon said good night to her at the door of the hotel. She put a hand on his arm to thank him, but suddenly he drew her into his arms and his lips were pressed down on hers before she could do anything to stop him.

Marlene pushed hard against him, but Ramon held her in a firm grip, and at the same time she became aware of a shadow in the light of the swing doors. She looked up and saw Juan just turning away. Anger gave her strength otherwise beyond her. She wrenched herself free, and without another word to Ramon hurtled herself through the revolving doors. But Juan had disappeared. She stood for a moment in the foyer. What would he think of her? After a few seconds she recovered from her tussle with Ramon, and as there was still no sign of Juan she went to the lift. What could she have said to him, anyway, which would make any difference? He wouldn't really be interested in whether Ramon kissed her or not.

She went unhappily to her flat and wished she had never come here.

In the post the following morning was a letter from Brenda saying that she and Molly would like to come and stay for a few days. A word with Juan and he said they could have a twin-bedded room next to his, if they would not mind sharing a room as at present only one room was available.

"I'm sure they wouldn't," Marlene told him. "And thank you."

"That's all right, and while they are here you must take some time off," he said.

"I will—for part of the day, anyway." She hesitated, wanting to explain to him about last night, to tell him that Ramon had kissed her without willingness on her part. But a look at his stern features and she decided against it. He would almost certainly tell her that she was free to do as she wished or did not wish, or even that it was no concern of his.

Marlene was very glad that a few days later Jane Saunders paid her a visit.

"If the mountain won't come to Mohammed, then Mohammed must come to the mountain," Jane said with a smile.

Marlene held out her hand. "Jane, how lovely to see you! I—I'm sorry I haven't been over to see you —but of course you're not on the phone, are you?"

"That needn't stop you. Come any time. I'll tell you a secret place where we keep the key, and if you come and we're out, you can make yourself a cup of tea. But we shall often be in Blanes in the summer, which is almost upon us, so I hope to see you often, and we can make a date to see you and Juan both."

Marlene's face clouded over. "I don't think you

should invite me and Juan together to anything, Jane."

"Why ever not?"

Marlene led the way up to her flat. "It's Frasquita and Juan you should invite."

Jane followed her into the kitchen where Marlene busied herself putting on the coffee percolator.

"What nonsense is this?" laughed Jane. "Frasquita and Juan? Never in a million years."

"I wouldn't be so sure, if I were you. I—I've seen them together. And why never in a million years? I should think they'd be admirably suited."

Jane continued to shake her head, but oddly enough she did not pursue the argument.

"As well as coming over to see you, I've come to visit the market."

"Market?"

"Yes. It's Whit Monday. There's always a market on Whit Monday, right along the sea-front." Jane gave her a closer look. "I should think an extra bit of sea air will do you good. You're not looking in either the best of health or spirits. Anything wrong?"

"Not really. At least, nothing that anybody can do anything about."

"Sounds serious. Shall I make a guess, or will you tell me?"

But Marlene shook her head. "I'd rather not talk about it, Jane, if you don't mind. Let's have our coffee and go out and see this market, shall we?"

"Fine. Then perhaps if you've nothing better to do you could take me to see your greenhouse and show me all your gardens. It must be wonderful to have a way with plants. Whenever I buy one it just dies on me."

Marlene smiled. "I'm quite sure you're exaggerating. All you have to do is find out what the natural needs of the plant are."

"Most times I don't even know a plant's name!" laughed Jane.

"No wonder the poor things die if you don't even know what they're called. You'll have to mend your ways, won't you?" quipped Marlene. "Start with a geranium. They're pretty tolerant—and I'll write you out some instructions."

Marlene found the market quite fascinating. The gay and colourful stalls were laid out the whole length of the Paseo del Mar. There was a happy, holiday atmosphere everywhere. Dark-haired youths and dark-eyed girls wandered in and out of the market stalls in groups, laughing and chatting, the Spanish stallholders beamed amiably in the warm, benevolent sunshine.

For no reason at all except that she could not resist the endearing expression on its face, Marlene bought a minute baby bull in black felt. Jane bought a *flamenco* dancer for Paul and Marlene also bought a set of castanets which included a lesson from the buxom stallholder on how to play them. There were brightly coloured beads, leather bags, dress materials, shawls and mantillas. It was something Marlene would not have missed for the world.

"What's Paul doing today?" she enquired.

"He's on the beach with his sailing dinghies," Jane told her. "Shall we go and have a word with him?"

They found him doing a very good trade, clad in a pair of shorts, his feet bare, in the warm sand, he was pushing off yet another pair of holidaymakers and the gently undulating sea was dotted with bobbing white sails.

"Like to try your hand?" he asked Marlene.

But Marlene was doubtful. "I've never sailed a boat in my life. I'd be scared out of my wits."

"Even with me?" said a familiar voice.

Marlene swung around to see a very unfamiliar

Juan dressed in a summer shirt and cream-coloured slacks.

Even Paul was surprised. "Juan, you old son-of-a-gun! It's not often we see you looking like a holiday-maker."

"Not often enough, perhaps," Juan conceded. Then he turned to Marlene. "Well, are you willing to risk half an hour with me in an open boat on an open sea?"

This was such a different person from the one she usually saw that she hardly knew what to say. He looked so English, she felt thrown off balance.

Paul laughed. "I don't think she can believe it's really you. All this time she has regarded you as the sedate and stern business man. Now, you almost look like a tourist. No wonder she's lost for words." He gave her a gentle push. "Go on, Marlene, you'll be all right. Juan can sail—I give you my word."

She allowed herself to be helped in the small yacht and was aware that Juan was helping Paul to push the vessel into the water.

"You're not really so scared, are you?" he asked as he jumped into the boat.

Marlene swallowed and shook her head. "Not now."

She loved him. How could she be afraid? He glanced up at the small flag on top of the mast, then gave the tiller a little push, jerked on a rope which controlled the sails, and all at once they were skimming through the water, the sails puffed out like a white balloon. Marlene held up her face and let the wind blow through her hair, feeling a strange exhilaration coursing through her veins.

"You like it?" asked Juan, glancing at her face.

"Mm, it's lovely. I've never done this before."

"I daresay there are quite a number of things you have never done before," he said, deftly missing another yacht which seemed to have lost wind.

"I daresay," she agreed, wondering what exactly he had in mind.

But suddenly her heart leapt in some alarm. They appeared to be heading straight for one of the coastal steamers which ferried passengers from one place along the coast to the other.

"Juan, look out!" she called.

But he kept on his course, greatly to her dismay. "Don't worry, it's all right," he told her.

Perhaps he thought the steamer would put on speed and be out of their course, but just as she was sure they would collide and find themselves in the water, Juan thrust the helm over and as the sails lost wind and flapped idly the yacht came almost to a stop.

"You see?" he said. "All you have to do is turn into wind. I hope I didn't frighten you."

Marlene swallowed. "I did think we might be heading for a collision."

He turned the yacht once more so that the sails filled out. "Did you really think I'd let that happen? You don't trust my judgement very much, do you?"

"Well, I—I thought perhaps—I mean—" At first, she had felt he was putting her on the spot, but as she spoke she realized she should have trusted him to know what he was doing. "I'm sorry, I should have known better. But we all make mistakes."

"Yes," he said soberly, "we do."

Was he referring to something else? she wondered. He seemed to be making a great issue out of a small incident.

They were in the wake of the steamer now and the small sailing boat was tossing rather too much for Marlene's liking. She would have preferred waters which were less busy. She hung rather desperately on to the sides of the boat.

"Too choppy for you?" Juan asked.

She tried to smile. "I'm sorry to be such a poor sailor. I was enjoying it at first—before the steamer came along. I think, on the whole, I'd prefer to sail on a lake or a river."

He nodded understandingly. "Sometimes the heavier traffic all seems to come at the same time. We'll go back now, and try again some other time."

She wondered if he was disappointed in her and felt miserable because she felt sure it must be so.

"Well, that was a short sail," Paul quipped as soon as they were back on the beach again. "What was the matter? Didn't you like it?"

It was Juan who answered. "She loved it, but it became a little too choppy for comfort with all the steamers which started to come and go."

Paul looked at him in surprise, but said no more, and Jane suggested that they should all go and get lunch somewhere.

The others agreed, and Paul called out to his assistant to take charge of things. It was odd, after what Marlene had said to Jane about not inviting Juan and herself together anywhere.

As busy as Blanes was with the market and it being a feast day, a table for four was miraculously found for them at the restaurant they entered. It was almost as if the whole thing had been planned and had not come about by chance at all. But by whom? Not Juan, she felt sure, and she hoped fervently that Jane and Paul were not trying any sort of matchmaking between herself and Juan. It would be too embarrassing when Juan himself did not want it.

When they were seated, she felt Jane's foot touch hers under the table.

"Cheer up, old thing. You're not attending somebody's funeral, you know," she murmured.

Marlene forced a smile that soon became a natural one as Paul and Jane, in particular, kept a bright conversation going. She thought Juan seemed happier today than she had seen him for some time, and wondered if this had anything to do with Frasquita.

After lunch Paul went back to his work and Juan to the hotel.

"And what is everyone doing this evening?" Paul asked before they split up. "Marlene?" he prompted as no one answered immediately.

Marlene hesitated. She wasn't doing anything in particular, but she still had a strong feeling that Paul and Jane were conspiring to bring Juan and herself together and was not at all happy about it.

"Is it a big secret?" Jane asked her.

Marlene looked from one to the other, suddenly aware that all three of them seemed to be waiting for her reply.

"Why pick on me?" she temporized. "What is everyone else doing?"

"As far as I'm concerned nothing special," declared Jane.

"That goes for me, too," Paul said.

Marlene caught a look from Juan and knew what he was thinking—that she might be seeing Ramon. For the first time she was tempted to lie and say she *was* seeing him. Oddly enough he had not asked her out this evening. He had mentioned it vaguely and said something about going to Barcelona to see El Cordobes, the matador. All the same, he often came to the hotel late in an evening unexpectedly, and as she felt sure Paul and Jane were trying gently to force Juan's hand regarding this evening, she decided to put them off. Juan was probably too polite to say he was seeing Frasquita. The Spanish held such odd views about these things.

"I'm sorry," she told the others, "but I'm not quite sure. I—I'd rather you didn't include me in any of your plans. I do hope you don't mind," she added, anxious not to offend Jane and Paul in particular.

Jane received this with obvious disappointment. Paul shrugged in the way men often do and Juan pushed back his chair and said he must be going. Marlene caught only a fleeting glimpse of his expression as he turned to leave the restaurant. There was silence between Jane and Marlene for a few minutes after the two men had gone. Jane fingered her coffee cup while Marlene thought desperately for something to say.

"Jane, I'm sorry," Marlene repeated at last. "I seem to have upset things. But I'm sure Juan didn't want to make up a foursome."

Jane sighed and shook her head. "You appear to have made up your mind about a good many things, Marlene, and I'm equally convinced that you're wrong about Juan."

"You forget, Jane. I see far more of Juan—and Frasquita—than you do. I'll be honest with you. I have a feeling you and Paul are trying a bit of old-fashioned matchmaking, and I don't think you should. It must be very embarrassing for Juan."

Jane laughed shortly. "Embarrassing my foot!"

"Well, it's embarrassing me."

"Nonsense," Jane said goodhumouredly.

"You admit you *are* conspiring, then?"

Jane gave an awkward smile. "Well, of course we are—just a little. We like you, and we're very fond of Juan. We think you'd be very suited to each other —in spite of you saying you'd never marry a Spaniard, or words to that effect. Juan isn't like other men. Anyway, what's wrong with friends trying to help things along if they can? Haven't you ever done something similar?"

Marlene gave her a startled look. Was it possible she knew about her own and Ramon's scheming on behalf of Frasquita? But she told herself it was impossible.

"It's altogether wrong, anyway," she answered. "And I must ask you, please, Jane, to stop it. I—happen to know that Frasquita is very much in love with Juan, and I have every reason to believe that he's at least beginning to fall in love with her."

Jane sighed. "All right, if you will insist on pairing them up. Time alone will tell whether or not you're right, though I still think you're making the biggest mistake of your life. Just tell me one thing, if you will. With whom are *you* in love?"

Marlene closed her eyes briefly and took a deep breath. "My feelings don't enter into it, except that I have no wish to be thrust into the arms of a man who doesn't want me. I've already had one humiliating experience and I don't want another, so if you don't mind, Jane, please stop your efforts on my behalf. And if you're wise you'll do the same for Juan."

Almost she added, *I only wish I hadn't interfered in his life*, but reasoned swiftly that even if she hadn't, that was not to say he would have fallen in love with herself.

Jane made no answer for a moment, then she said: "I hope I haven't really offended you, Marlene. That's the last thing either Paul or I wanted to do."

"No, no, of course not." Marlene reassured her. "Let's go and take a look at the gardens, if you're still interested. We'll leave Pineda until the last—the Hotel del Jardin, that is. Then perhaps we can have tea there. It's a lovely hotel."

Paul had parked his car nearby, and so after a word with him Jane used it to run Marlene and herself to Juan's various hotels.

Jane was rather quiet as they drove first to Lloret to see the hotel there, and Marlene feared she had spoken too sharply when she had asked Jane to stop trying to bring Juan and herself together. So she apologized, and to make further amends and help Jane to understand Marlene told her something about Roger.

"Of course I'm well over it now. It helped, coming to Spain, but it isn't a very pleasant experience being dropped by a man for someone else. Next time—if there is a next time—I shall want to be very, very sure indeed that a man really loves me before I—before I let him get an inkling of my feelings for him."

Jane responded immediately with warm sympathy. "I can well understand how you feel. An experience like that will naturally make you cautious."

Marlene laughed ironically. "The funny thing is, he's now broken it off—or she has. There seems some doubt as to which way it happened."

"Ah! Don't tell me he wants you back now."

"I don't know. Maybe. He asked a friend of mine for my address."

"Did you tell her to give it to him?"

Marlene shook her head. "I didn't tell her not to, either, but I haven't heard from him."

"I wonder why you didn't tell her not to?" mused Jane.

"I don't know."

"Perhaps deep in your subconscious you *wanted* to hear from him—and to see him again."

Marlene shook her head. "I hardly think so."

For a while she puzzled her mind, trying to think why she had not asked Brenda not to give Roger her address. Then she realized that in actual fact she had forgotten to mention it at all. Whether Roger would be all that persistent and she would give way to him and let him have it was a matter for speculation. At any rate she had not heard from him. She said nothing more on the subject, however. She knew Jane was trying to find out—in the nicest way—whether or not she was still in love with Roger and was trying to find out her feelings for Juan. But it was best if Jane did not know the truth. She might, quite inadvertently, of course, let it slip out to Juan, and Marlene did not want that.

The front of the hotel at Lloret far outshone its neighbours in the brilliancy of its flowers. Marlene saw this with new eyes as Jane stood and exclaimed her admiration. The front of the hotel where small tables and chairs were set out had the blue flowers of morning glory climbing up its white walls, tubs containing scarlet geraniums were in full bloom and an air even of graciousness was added by potted palms and the grevillea and other foliage plants, all of which had been a gardener's dream in the rapid progress they had made in this benign climate.

"Of course I'm well used to seeing roses and geraniums in full flower out of doors in the spring here, at least two months ahead of everything at home," said Jane. "But I must say in the short time you've been here, you've worked wonders. Miracles even."

Marlene laughed, "Well, it's nice to be appreciated, anyway!"

"You're not meaning that Juan doesn't appreciate your efforts?"

"Of course not, though I must say he hasn't quite your enthusiastic way of expressing things."

"What sort of things does he say?"

"Oh—'it looks good', or 'you've done well'."

"Typical masculine understatements," observed Jane.

She was even more enthusiastic when she saw the gardens in Pineda.

"And you grew all these marvellous plants yourself from seeds?" she exclaimed as she saw the full and colourful greenhouse as well as those in the garden and around the swimming pool.

"Oh yes. It's quite easy, really."

"Well, I wish you'd show me how. Seeing all you've done makes me feel I'd like to try."

"Why not try your hand at growing some cinerarias to flower indoors in the winter?" Marlene suggested.

"Cinerarias? What are those?"

Marlene laughed. "Heavens, Jane, don't you know anything? Cinerarias are those daisy-like flowers you used to see in all the florists around January. They come in a wide range of colours—blue, pinks, red, orange. You can have them in flower by December, but I suspect most of the florists keep them back around Christmas so as to sell the more expensive poinsettias and azaleas. Anyway, here's what you do."

She filled a small seed pan with fine moist soil and sprinkled a dozen or so seeds on the surface, then just covered them with soil.

"Give them a good drink of water from this watering can with the fine hose, cover them with something to keep the moisture in and prevent drying out, then put them in a warm shady place. Look at them every day, and as soon as the first seedling begins to show take off the cover, but still keep in light shade, not full sun. Then when they've got about four leaves transplant them to small individual pots and put them outside in a shady place. Let me show you where I've got mine."

She took Jane outside to where, in the shade of a shrub, she had several large trays full of seedlings in small pots.

"It's the planting out that would defeat me," Jane said doubtfully.

"When the time comes I'll show you," Marlene promised. "And then perhaps you'll show me how to paint pictures," she added, feeling she had aired her own knowledge quite enough.

"With pleasure," Jane told her.

There were comparatively few guests in and around the hotel. Some would naturally be on the beach, while others would no doubt have gone to Blanes or Barcelona.

"There's a good market here in Pineda every Friday, isn't there?" Jane said as they sat in the garden beside the pool having tea. "Shall we make a date for next Friday and come? It's always nicer having someone to look around with."

Marlene agreed. She had been in Spain quite a number of weeks before she had discovered the market at Pineda and even then had had only a brief look around, not wanting to lose any time away from her work. But now she could afford to slow down a little and so she made the date with Jane.

By the time they had gone the rounds of the other hotels it was almost seven o'clock.

"Paul will wonder what's keeping me." Jane said as she drove back to where she had picked up the car "But as it's a *fiesta* he might still be busy."

When they reached the place where his boats were moored, however, he was not there. He had left word with his assistant that he had gone to the Hotel Marina and would wait for her there.

Jane drove them the short distance, and as they came in sight of the hotel Marlene began to feel uneasy and not a little conscience-stricken at having declined to spend the evening with the other three. Juan would quite probably invite Jane and Paul to stay to dinner, and if she herself did not join them it would look most unfriendly. As to Ramon, he might not put in an appearance at all this evening.

When they entered the hotel they found Paul sitting on a high stool at the cocktail bar. Juan was in the dining room supervising the serving of dinner to the guests. From where she was standing when they joined Paul Marlene could see him, and she was struck by an unusually grave look on his face.

"There are some visitors for you, Marlene," Paul told her.

"Visitors? But I don't know anybody."

"They're from England."

Understanding dawned upon her. "Good heavens! It must be Molly and Brenda. But I wasn't expecting them for another two or three days. Where are they?"

"In the lounge. I can see them from where I'm sitting. One of them might be Brenda or Molly, but the other—take a look."

Startled, Marlene changed her position and looked. To her utter astonishment and consternation it was Roger who sat there, and with him was Brenda.

CHAPTER NINE

MARLENE'S consternation changed to anger as she went into the lounge to speak to the pair. Roger rose to his feet as she approached, an easy smile on his face. Brenda looked decidedly uncomfortable and there was mute pleading in her blue eyes.

For a moment Marlene felt too angry even to greet Roger. "Hello, Brenda," she said. "What's happened to Molly?"

"She—she couldn't come at the last minute. Roger had some free time and said he'd like to come, so—so he came. I did write to you, but they—they say they weren't expecting us."

Marlene took a deep breath. "We were expecting you and Molly in a couple of days' time—and I certainly haven't received a letter telling me that Roger was coming."

Roger eyed her with some amusement. "Well, now that I am here, aren't you even going to speak to me?"

Marlene looked at him coldly. "Roger, you had no right to come here uninvited, and I must ask you to leave again as soon as possible."

His eyes opened wide. "But this is a hotel, isn't it? I have every right to come here, and to stay, if the proprietor has a vacancy."

"You have that right, certainly, but please don't regard yourself as my guest. My invitation was for Molly and Brenda, and Señor de Montserrat kindly offered them a room with twin beds. I hope you didn't introduce yourself to him as my friend?"

Roger grimaced and inclined his head. "I left the

talking to Brenda."

Marlene turned angry eyes to Brenda, who was still looking decidedly uncomfortable.

"I—I'm sorry, Marlene, truly, but I honestly didn't think you would mind. I wrote to you almost a week ago. I thought if you had any objections to Roger coming instead of Molly you'd send a cable or something."

Marlene found her anger melting. "Even if you did write to me a week ago, that wasn't giving me much time to reply, was it?" she said in a gentler tone.

"So are you going to say hello to me properly and say you're pleased to see me?" put in Roger swiftly.

"No, I am not going to say I'm pleased to see you," she said firmly, "because I'm not."

He shrugged. "Well, I can't say I blame you after what I did. That's one reason I wanted to come—to ask you if you've forgiven me."

Marlene sighed. "I don't want to talk about the past, Roger. It's over and done with. I can't prevent you from staying here, as you say, but I must ask you to make your own arrangements with Señor de Montserrat while I show Brenda to her room. Come along, Brenda. I'll see him myself later."

On the way upstairs Brenda apologized once again. "You see, Roger said he was coming over in any case," she explained. "I don't drive, as you know. Molly was going to do the driving. So if I hadn't come with Roger, I wouldn't have been able to come at all—at least, not for some time."

"What's wrong with Molly?"

"She fell downstairs and broke her leg. It was her idea, really, that I should come with Roger, and between the two of them I allowed myself to be persuaded. Molly felt sure you'd still be in love with Roger and that you'd be pleased to see him. You aren't, are you?"

"Still in love with him? No, I'm not."

"He is with you, you know."

Marlene laughed shortly. "I doubt it. I doubt if he ever was."

She showed Brenda the room which was to have been hers and Molly's, then took her into the flat. As Marlene had been herself, Brenda was enchanted with the flat and went into raptures at the sight of the magnificent view of the bay.

"How marvellous of him to have given you this super flat. Do you like him?"

"He's all right. But I don't think I'm going to stay for another season." As she spoke she was conscious of a real stab of pain and knew that leaving this place and Juan would be an agony to her. Yet she must. She must.

Brenda eyed her in frank astonishment. "Not stay— in a place as marvellous as this? Why ever not?"

But Marlene was not to be drawn. She did not want anyone to know how she felt about Juan, especially, perhaps, Brenda, who was well known for not being able to keep a secret.

"I don't want to talk about it, Brenda. I expect you'd like some tea, wouldn't you? I'll make a cup."

Brenda followed her into the kitchen, chattering away, telling Marlene all the news of mutual friends back home.

It was while they were drinking the tea that the house telephone rang in the flat. It was Juan.

"Marlene, would you mind coming down to the office for a few minutes?" he asked. "I want to talk to you."

"Yes, of course. I'll be right down."

He wanted to know why it was that Roger had come instead of Molly, without a doubt. Marlene promised Brenda to have her luggage sent up, then went downstairs, her heart beginning to quicken its beat.

Juan was in the office alone, his face drawn tight. "This young man Roger Hetherington," he said without preliminary. "He's the son of Lord Hetherington, I take it?"

"That's right. I—I'm sorry about his turning up unexpectedly. My other friend, Molly, has had an accident and couldn't come. Roger had decided to come to Spain at this particular time, so she travelled with him."

"So." His expression relaxed. "You did not know he was coming. You must have known him very well —a special friend, perhaps?"

"You could say that, but—"

"I suspect he came specially to see you."

Marlene could not give a decidedly negative answer to that, so she made no reply. Juan gave her a penetrating look.

"Very well, I have a staff room vacant now, as it happens. He shall be your guest."

But Marlene shook her head swiftly. "I would prefer that he was not my guest, if you don't mind."

"Then he shall be mine. If he is a friend of yours, I cannot possibly take money from him." Marlene opened her lips to protest, but Juan held up his hand. "No more arguments. The matter is closed. You and they can either take your meals in the restaurant or our dining room, whichever you prefer. And, of course, take all the time off you want while they are here."

He began to turn over some papers, and Marlene felt herself dismissed. She went out of the office distinctly put out by this turn of events. Why had Roger done this? It was unforgivable of him. Surely he did not expect to pick up their relationship where it had been before he had broken off their engagement?

At the foot of the lift she hesitated. She supposed she ought, at least, to ask him up to her flat for a cup of tea. But she hated the idea, and her anger rose once more at the position in which he had placed her by his coming. She had been looking forward to seeing Molly and Brenda. Now—

Suddenly Roger appeared, and preceding him was Manuel, who was carrying two large suitcases with additional grips under each arm.

Still angry, Marlene asked Manuel which floor he wanted, and they all went up to the fourth where her flat was situated.

"Where's Brenda?" asked Roger as they stepped out.

Marlene sighed. Now that he was here she could scarcely escape seeing something of him, she supposed.

"She's in my flat having a cup of tea. Perhaps you'd like one, too," she answered.

He grinned. "Ah, now that's better!"

He followed her in and, as Brenda had done, made appreciative remarks about both the view and her pleasant quarters, though not in quite the same language.

"Montserrat has done you proud—obviously wants to make sure you stay," he remarked.

Marlene did not answer. Instead she asked: "When did you both last eat—at lunchtime?"

Brenda nodded. "I don't know about Roger, but I'm starving. But thanks for the tea, it was lovely."

"Well, I suggest we tidy up and go down to dinner. They're serving it now in the restaurant. You can use my bathroom, Brenda. I think there's one at the end of the corridor you can use, Roger."

This, she thought later as they were seated in the restaurant, solved her problem of how she should spend the rest of the evening, though in a way she had never dreamed of.

"Is this where you usually have your meals?" Roger enquired.

Marlene shook her head and told him about the set-up. "But I shall probably have my meals in here with you and Brenda while you are here. At least, the evening meal. Don't count on me at lunchtime, though. I have it wherever I happen to be at the time. I shall have to leave you both to your own devices in the main. I'm a working girl, don't forget."

"But don't you take any time off?"

"Naturally, but my work comes first."

From time to time during the meal Marlene caught sight of Juan, and once he came to their table to ask if they were enjoying their meal. Of Frasquita there was no sign, and Marlene concluded that she was having an evening off.

Surprisingly, Ramon came into the hotel later. Marlene was sitting in the lounge with Roger and Betty. She did not want Roger to acquire the habit of using her flat as a sitting room. She wanted to keep their relationship as distant as possible. When Ramon saw them he naturally joined them, and Marlene introduced Roger and Betty.

Ramon was even more charming than usual. A new face stimulated him, it seemed. And clearly, Brenda was intrigued with the handsome Spaniard. Before long Roger looked bored and asked Marlene to come for a walk along the sea-front. Marlene hesitated. She didn't really want to. She would have preferred to go up to her flat. But Roger said :

"Just for five minutes. There's something I want to talk to you about."

His voice had taken on a serious note. Marlene rose. If there were things he wanted to say to her she might as well let him get it over. She slipped upstairs for a wrap and they went out together. Juan saw them go, and Marlene thought wryly to herself that he would no doubt come to the conclusion that Roger was an ex-boy-friend and that they were making up a lovers' quarrel.

They strolled beneath the trees along the brightly lighted Paseo Maestranza in silence for a little while, then they sat down on one of the seats.

"Well, Roger, what was it you wanted to talk to me about?" Marlene prompted him.

He took her hand, but she firmly withdrew it. "You're finding it very hard to forgive me, aren't you?" he asked with regret in his voice.

"It's not a question of forgiving you, Roger. It's simply all over between us, that's all."

"I never loved Caroline, you do realize that, don't you? I've never loved anyone but you."

Marlene rose swiftly to her feet. "I don't want to talk about it, Roger. You broke off our engagement to marry someone else, and whatever my feelings were at the time I have quite recovered from them now."

"In so short a time?"

"It wasn't easy, Roger, but there's nothing so dead as dead love."

She began to walk back to the hotel and he fell into step beside her. Then suddenly, oblivious of passers-by, he swung her round to face him and grasped her by the shoulders.

"Marlene, are you sure that it's as dead as all that?"

She wrenched herself free, suddenly wanting to cry as heartbreaking memories came rushing back into her mind and heart to mingle with her present unhappiness on Juan's account. She found herself longing for his love with an intensity she had not felt before.

"Please, Roger, I don't want to talk about it."

She started to run without knowing quite why. To get away from Roger, perhaps, but more in an effort to run away from herself and the tumult within her.

When she re-entered the hotel, Brenda was nowhere to be seen. Jane and Paul were on the point of leaving and told her that Brenda had gone off somewhere with Ramon.

Jane's discerning look took in Marlene's heightened colour, the breathlessness which she was striving to control. "Marlene, are you all right?" she queried anxiously.

"Yes. Yes, I'm all right. I—I'll see you Friday, Jane. Let's meet at the Hotel del Jardin for coffee about eleven, then we'll go to the market."

It was agreed, and Jane and Paul said good night. Marlene bade Roger a brief good night and went towards the lift, but he followed her and they went up in the lift together. Outside the door of her flat he grasped her by the shoulders again.

"Darling, why did you run away?" he asked in a gentle voice.

Her eyes blazed angrily. "Because I wanted to get away from you. Don't you understand? Let me go!"

But he held her the more firmly and his masculine strength was too much for her. Marlene caught a glimpse of a light under Juan's door and expected him any moment to come out to see what was happening.

Roger tried to kiss her. She avoided his searching lips, but he still had her arms pinioned to her sides. Desperately, in case Juan should open his door and find her like this, she had a sudden idea. She ceased struggling and went limp, and as she had hoped Roger relaxed his hold on her a little.

"That's better," he murmured. "Now kiss me, and then tell me that you don't love me."

She brought her face round to his with the pretence

of complying, then as his arms relaxed still further she gave him a sudden push which sent him almost off his balance.

"I don't want to kiss you, and I don't love you," she said vehemently, keeping her voice as low as possible. "Now will you please leave me alone, or I shall ask Juan to throw you out!"

She went swiftly into her room and turned the key in the lock against the possibility of his trying to follow her, then sank on the bed exhausted by all the events of the day and the depth of her emotions. Did Roger *really* love her? she wondered. If he was sincere, then she should feel a fellow-sympathy for him. But how ironical, if so, that she could have one man's love for the taking, yet the one she really wanted was denied her.

She was almost asleep when there came a gentle tap on her door. Remembering that the key was still turned in the lock, Marlene switched on the light, slipped into a négligée and opened the door to admit Brenda.

"Hope I haven't wakened you up," whispered Brenda.

"No, I wasn't quite asleep," Marlene assured her, glancing at her watch. It was eleven-thirty, not late by Spanish standards. "Where did you and Ramon get to?" she asked.

Brenda dropped into a chair, her eyes bright with excitement.

"I hope you didn't mind. He took me to one of those *bodega* places—you know."

"Yes, I know. It's probably the same one to which he took me."

Brenda eyed her anxiously. "You and he weren't—"

Marlene shook her head. "Friends, that's all."

"Oh, good. I think he's super. I've arranged to see

170

him tomorrow night."

"Fine," Marlene told her. "But watch that you don't go overboard for him."

"Why?"

"No real reason, except that he strikes me as being something of a playboy."

"Well, he's fun, anyway. But what about you and Roger? Did you—talk things over?"

"We did—and I'd like you to do something for me, Brenda."

"If I can. What is it?"

"Keep him out of my hair—at least during the day. If you're going to see much of Ramon I only hope Roger makes friends with one or two of the English girls staying at the hotel."

"It's definitely over between you and him, then?"

"Definitely."

Marlene had intended taking some time off during the current week, especially as she had been expecting Molly and Brenda within a few days, but to avoid encountering Roger too often she kept busy, spending most of her time at Pineda. Each evening as soon as she had had dinner she went straight up to her room and spent the rest of the evening watching television and studying Spanish.

She need not have worried about the attentions of Roger. After the first evening he found a vacant place at a table with two young girls. Once, Brenda and herself were joined at dinner by Ramon, and on several other evenings he took Brenda out to dinner. As far as possible Marlene avoided coming into contact with Juan, too. When she did see him either in the office or some other part of the hotel she fancied he looked a little sterner than usual.

"You know what's happening at the Hotel Marina while you're keeping so busy, don't you?" Jane said to her when they met for coffee on the Friday as arranged.

"I don't know what you mean," Marlene answered. "I do know that Ramon is taking Brenda around, but as far as I'm concerned—"

"It's not Brenda and Ramon I'm talking about. It's Roger and Frasquita."

Marlene drew in a startled breath. "Roger and Frasquita? Oh no!"

"Oh yes," corrected Jane. "And what's more, she seems to like him." She looked at Marlene's distressed face. "This Roger—he's the one you told me about?"

Marlene stared at her. "What does that matter? It's Juan I'm concerned about."

Jane gave an exasperated sigh. "How often must I tell you, Marlene? Juan is not in love with Frasquita."

"But how can you possibly speak with such conviction, Jane? He must be. No wonder he's been grim these last few days."

"If Juan is looking grim it's on your account. He's guessed that Roger is an old flame of yours, that you were once engaged, in fact, and thinks he's come to patch things up."

"And so that's why he's taking Frasquita out? Really!"

"Maybe he thinks Roger is doing it to make you jealous."

"That might be true of Frasquita, but I've made it very plain to Roger that as far as I'm concerned there's absolutely nothing between us. Frankly, I think he's pretty much the same kind of man as Ramon. There's very little depth to their love."

"But you *were* once engaged to Roger."

"People differ in their conception of love. Why he came here I simply don't know."

"I expect he thought you might still be in love with

him, especially as it was he who broke off the engagement. I expect you *were* still in love with him for a time."

"Yes, but not any more," Marlene told her with quiet conviction.

"Because you're in love with Juan?"

Marlene stiffened. Then she sighed deeply and relaxed. It was useless, obviously, trying to keep the fact from Jane.

"How did you guess?"

Jane laughed. "You went to such pains to avoid being paired up with him. Besides, my womanly intuition told me something was making you miserable, though——" She broke off, then said brightly: "Come along, let's go and have a look round the market. Maybe that will cheer you up a little."

"You—won't let it slip to Juan—or give him any hint as to how I feel about him?"

"I'll leave that to you—only for heaven's sake stop running away from him!"

They strolled up and down the gay, colourful market and stopped every now and then to admire the fantastically dressed dolls, the beautifully embroidered linens and the pottery and lingered at the stalls selling herbs and spices. But part of Marlene's mind was occupied with thoughts of Juan, thinking over some of the things Jane had said. Could she really be right about his not being in love with Frasquita? At first the idea thrilled her, but she sobered as she realized that this did not mean he had any particular regard for herself.

"Jane," she said suddenly, "how do you know all this—about Frasquita going out with Roger?"

"What?" Jane dragged her attention away from the gaily-patterned materials. "Oh, Juan came over to see us one day."

"Are you sure he wasn't upset about Frasquita?"

"Quite sure. He was worried on your behalf."

"I can't understand Frasquita," Marlene said reflectively, her mind going back to the tempestuous scene in the office when Frasquita had displayed her jealousy so passionately. "She was so desperately in love with Juan."

"Well, you know what emotional people they can be. The women of this country are so hidebound by convention. Things are almost bound to simmer underneath, and get out of proportion, too."

"But Ramon confided to me that she was, too. He even got me to—" She broke off, feeling she was saying too much.

But Jane darted a swift look at her. "You mean he got you to help him to bring them together, and then you discovered you loved him yourself? Oh, Marlene!"

Marlene laughed ironically. "Ridiculous, isn't it?"

"It's more than ridiculous."

Marlene frowned. "But there's something else. Frasquita is breaking all her country's conventions if she's going out with Roger alone. It's a wonder Ramon approves."

Jane shook her head and sighed. "Look, Marlene, what are you trying to prove to yourself? Maybe the conventions are not as strict as you think among the young in this day and age. Maybe Ramon and Brenda go with them. But why don't you stick around the hotel a little more? You might find out more about what's happening."

There was still much which puzzled Marlene, however. She couldn't believe that Frasquita could so quickly turn to Roger, unless—unless Juan himself had made it plain that he had no affection for her. And then there were these mysterious trips into the mountains. He had been twice quite recently. Whom did he visit?

That evening Marlene encountered Ramon in the hotel waiting for Brenda.

"Your little friend is quite charming," he told her. "But why did you quarrel with Roger? He, too, is a charming man. Frasquita is quite taken with him."

"Oh, really? What about Juan?" she asked him.

He shrugged. "Maybe when he sees Frasquita has eyes for someone else he will realize what he is missing. It pleases me that she has found another admirer."

"And—and has Juan shown any signs of jealousy?" she asked.

"Who can tell what he is thinking? Something is certainly bugging him, as you English say."

"Are you having dinner with Brenda this evening?" she asked him.

He nodded. "In the restaurant here with Roger and Frasquita."

"I see."

Marlene went upstairs thoughtfully, thinking of Juan. Tonight she would dine with him. She dressed, taking extra care with her appearance, and went downstairs while dinner in the restaurant was still in progress. She sat at the cocktail bar where Juan would see her when he had finished supervising the meal, then went into the small dining room. After a few minutes Juan entered.

"Well, well," he exclaimed. "Am I to have the honour of your company at dinner this evening?"

"If I'm not intruding."

He smiled a little ironically. "Not in the least. I may say I've been somewhat neglected of late. Deserted, almost. What will you have to drink?"

Her hand was shaking a little as she took a glass of sherry from him.

"I've been deserted, rather, too."

He gave her a long look. "So I have observed. I'm sorry."

"I don't mind," she told him. "In fact I'm rather glad. I didn't ask him to come. I didn't *want* him to come. And I didn't want to have to spend time with him out of politeness."

"I take it you're referring to Roger?"

"That's right."

"And what about Ramon? You don't mind your friend commandeering him?"

"Not in the slightest," she assured him.

She watched him carefully and saw him relax.

"Well, I'm glad you're not being made unhappy by either of them," he said.

Micaela brought in their meal and as they ate Juan talked about the tourist trade and the various problems of the business. Marlene was surprised at this, and had to confess to herself to being a little disappointed. His reaction to what she had told him had been no more than ordinary relief that at least she was not being made miserable by either of the two men.

Then quite suddenly when they were drinking their coffee together, he said:

"Marlene, will you come with me tomorrow to a place near Montserrat? There's someone I'd like you to meet."

CHAPTER TEN

He gave no further explanation and, sensing he wanted to give none at this stage, Marlene did not ask him any questions. Indeed, he seemed not to want to talk at all. He played some music and listened in silence. Marlene took her cue from him, partly listening to the music and partly wondering who it was he wanted her to meet and why. Not his parents. He had told her he had none. Then whom? Not, surely, a fiancée? Wife? She glanced at his face—either deep in thought or submerged in the music—and rejected the idea. Then she recalled that he had been talking of buying a house. It was hardly likely that he would build or buy a house in which simply to live alone. Perhaps tomorrow would supply some of the answers.

"What time do you want to leave for Montserrat tomorrow?" she asked when one piece of music came to an end.

He started out of his thoughts. "Would nine o'clock suit you?"

"Of course." She rose then. "If you will excuse me, Juan, I think I shall go to bed."

He rose with her and switched off the record player. "Have you a large straw hat? Part of the journey will be hot and I shall take an open car. But take, also, a warm sweater or jacket. It can be cool high in the mountain and we may be late coming back."

She had bought a straw hat for wearing when she was doing garden work outside and it was still fairly presentable. She said good night to him and went up to her room, greatly intrigued that he should ask her to accompany him, and filled with a subdued excitement. One other fact stood out clearly for her. He had not seemed upset in the slightest that Frasquita was spending time with Roger. Was it possible that she could hope, after all? Or would it be best if she went back to her own country and so avoid even greater unhappiness? Could she bear seeing him every day, loving him but not being loved by him in return? Even if he were not in love with Frasquita there was always a possibility that such a man would marry sooner or later.

For a long time that night Marlene lay awake tossing about, unable to come to any clear decision as to the future, and when she did at last fall asleep it was to dream that she was lost in the mountains and was calling out to Juan to come and find her.

She was awakened at eight o'clock by Micaela bearing her breakfast tray.

"But, Micaela, I didn't ask you—"

Micaela flashed her a smile. "Señor de Montserrat, he tell me."

"I see. Well, thank you very much, Micaela."

How kind and thoughtful he was! A great love and tenderness flooded Marlene's heart. Micaela went out silently, and as the door closed behind her Marlene suddenly realized that she had been almost afraid even to *feel* her love for him. Now she stopped being afraid, and as she allowed the great love she had for him to sink ever more deeply into her heart and mind she knew a tremendous sense of peace and happiness. Love like this, whether it was returned or not, was not something to shrink from or be afraid of. She should embrace it and be thankful for it, embrace and nurture it.

After some thought she decided to wear a little suit

in a tiny navy and white check with white collar and cuffs. Under the jacket she wore a white sleeveless blouse, and over her arm she carried a navy blue blazer against the cold about which Juan had warned her. He was waiting for her in the hotel foyer when she came down and noticed his glance of approval at her choice of dress.

"I see you have the hat to match," he said in jest, as he caught sight of the navy straw hat she carried.

"Purely coincidence," she told him. Then: "Thank you for having my breakfast sent up. It was very thoughtful of you."

They went out to the car. "I wanted you to have a decent breakfast—not just throw down a cup of coffee or nibble at a roll," he said.

"Are you trying to bully me?" she asked happily.

The corners of his lips curved into a smile. "Someone has to speak to you for your own good."

"And who speaks to you for your good?" she ventured to retaliate as he drove out of the courtyard.

He inclined his head. "I fear no one does. But hope, as the saying goes, springs eternal."

She simply dared not ask him what he meant by that. The obvious answer was that he hoped one day to have a wife who would take on the task, but he might not have meant it as seriously as all that.

The mountain of Montserrat was inland from Barcelona. Juan took the coast road to the city, drove through its busy streets and out again, going in a northerly direction. For quite a time he kept to the main road which gradually climbed as the distant mountain came into view. Soon the jagged peaks which had given the mountain its name could be seen, and it was then that Juan left the busy main road. After another few minutes' driving he stopped the car beside a swiftly flowing river, suggesting it was time for some refreshment. He spread out a rug on the grass and reached out a picnic basket from the rear seat of the car.

"I suppose you know that the name Montserrat means 'saw-tooth mountain'," he said as they drank coffee from a thermos flask.

"I read it somewhere," she told him. "It's called that because of its jagged peaks—and has a famous monastery over a thousand years old." Then a thought struck her which, oddly enough, had never done so before. "How strange that you should bear the same name."

"Thereby hangs a tale," he said gravely. "I shall tell it to you before the day is out, but not yet. Tell me, would you have married Ramon if he had asked you?"

The suddenness of the question brought a gasp of surprise from her.

"Heavens, no. What a question!"

"But why not? He's handsome, charming—and is certainly not poor."

Marlene laughed. "I never even knew what he did for a living. And I wouldn't have married him, for the simple reason that I was never in love with him."

"Were you not, perhaps, when you first came here, still in love with Roger?"

"I suppose so. At least, I was still—shall we say—hurt. But I'm definitely not in love with him now—and certainly not with Ramon. I thought I'd already said so."

"But for the sake of proving a point; if you *had* been in love with Ramon and he had asked you to marry him, would you have done so?"

She stared at him. "It's a little hard to imagine, but yes, I expect so. Why do you ask?"

"Several reasons. One is, that having regard to some

of our past conversations about the place of women in Spanish society, I am curious to know whether, in fact, you would ever even consider marrying a man of this country."

If it were you—oh, yes, yes, yes, she said to herself, still puzzled as to why he wanted to know.

"If—if I loved a man of this country sufficiently—yes," she answered him.

"*Any* man?" he pressed.

A small area of pain was beginning to make itself felt in her heart. Why, why, why was he asking?

She swallowed hard and said without looking at him : "Not *any* man. *One* man. You said you had several reasons for asking these things. May I know what the others are?"

"One other is that I want to keep you here," he said.

The bright sunny day suddenly clouded over for her. Tears came into her eyes and she felt an uncomfortable restriction in her throat. So that was why he was asking? He did not want to lose a good employee. She bit her lip and began to gather up the picnic things.

"You—you're asking too much," she said in a tight voice.

He did not answer. He rose to his feet as she had done and began to fold up the rug on which they had been sitting. He put both the picnic basket and the rug into the back of the car then came to where Marlene was standing gazing out at the jagged sawtooth mountain and trying to bring her feelings under control. She felt his arm across her shoulders and stiffened, recalling the way he had done the same thing to Frasquita.

Sensing her stiffen, he dropped his arm again and she turned to go and sit in the car. But suddenly he grasped her by both shoulders and brought her round to face him.

"Marlene, would you marry me?"

Her eyes widened as she looked at him and a panic began to stir in her heart.

"Marry you? Why? Just because you want to keep me here to look after your plants? Oh, but I forgot. I should be expected to stay at home. Or do you think because I'm English I would be happy to continue working and you would not mind flaunting your country's conventions?"

She wrenched away from him and went to the door of the car, wishing with all her heart that she had never agreed to come with him on this trip. Whom did he wish her to meet? More English friends so that she would be induced to stay in Spain? Her thoughts raced on.

"Marlene!"

The note of command in his voice caused her to halt instinctively. He came towards her again.

"Marlene—" he said again in a more gentle tone. "Why do you run away from me? I will ask you once again. Will you marry me?"

"But—but, Juan, why? Why do you want to marry me?"

His expression softened in a way which made her feel weak and limp.

"Why?" he repeated wonderingly. "Because I love you, of course."

Her heart gave a great leap. She gazed at him wide-eyed, unable to believe what she had just heard him say.

"Juan—" she said at last. "Oh, Juan!" She did not know whether to laugh or cry. "Do—do you really mean it?"

For answer he put his arms about her and kissed

her full upon her trembling lips, and she knew a world of ecstasy she had never felt before in her whole life.

"Well?" he asked gently, after a moment or two. "What is your answer now?"

Her eyes swimming with tears of happiness, she laughed, "Oh yes, yes, of course I will!"

"Even with all the conventions and taboos of a Spanish marriage—a woman's place being in the home and all that?" he queried in a gently mocking voice.

"I love you," she answered simply. "I love you, Juan."

He took a deep breath and crushed her to him with sudden vehemence, kissing her in a way which left her in no doubt about the depth of his feelings for her.

"Oh, Juan, I can hardly believe it," she whispered when at last he released her.

"Neither can I," he answered, cupping her face in his hands and letting his eyes flick over her features. "Only the fact that you cared nothing for Ramon and had ceased to care for Roger gave me courage. But come. We must continue our journey. Later, we can talk and make plans."

As Juan left the road on which they had been travelling for even narrower ones which wound up and up and were little more than paths in places, Marlene wondered how on earth he would find his way back.

"Is this the place you visit periodically?" she asked him.

He nodded. "I was brought up from a boy among these mountain paths. I know every inch."

After they had been driving for some time they came out on to a sort of plateau where sheep grazed on the sparse grass, and in the distance a shepherd wearing an old leather jacket and a little skull cap.

As they drew near him Juan stopped the car. The shepherd came towards them, a broad smile on his rough, weatherbeaten face.

"Juan, my boy, welcome."

Juan got out of the car and shook hands with him, then turned to Marlene.

"Marlene, I want you to meet my foster-father, Miguel—Miguel Abadesas."

"Your foster-father?" exclaimed Marlene involuntarily.

Miguel held out a brown hand and Marlene shook hands with him. Juan spoke to him in rapid Spanish, and Miguel gave a broad smile.

"*Bueno, bueno.*"

Miguel got in the back of the car and Juan drove a little further where, in the shelter of a group of rocks, stood a small square hamlet. As they drew up a sweet-faced woman almost as wrinkled and weatherbeaten as Miguel appeared at the door.

"Marlene," Juan said when they approached the woman, "this is my foster-mother, Maria."

Marlene shook hands and again there was an exchange of greetings and news in Spanish. Then Maria bade them enter.

The interior of the place was dimly lit by means of only one small window containing no glass and the open door, but in a very short time Marlene's eyes became accustomed to the gloom and she could see a clean and tidy room, sparsely furnished. In the centre of the room was a table set with a clean tablecloth, and it was evident that they were expected to lunch.

Maria moved about quietly casting an occasional smile in Marlene's direction, and soon they were invited to sit at the table. Juan spoke partly in English and partly in Spanish, acting as interpreter for both languages when necessary. Neither Miguel nor Maria could speak English, and though Marlene could pick out a word or phrase here and there from the old couple they spoke in a dialect which was difficult to understand.

There was a simple, natural dignity about the couple, and Marlene could not help wondering why they never visited Blanes, or how it was that Juan had chosen a life so different from theirs. But this highland shepherd and his wife were his foster-parents only. What had happened to his real parents? she pondered as they ate.

It was a simple meal of soup with croutons, chicken and rice and fruit accompanied by a wine which tasted like champagne.

When they had finished eating Marlene wanted to help to clear away, but Maria would not hear of it. She made coffee and they grouped their chairs in the doorway and talked. It was mainly, Marlene gathered, about the weather and sheep and the state of things in agriculture and simple philosophizing. After a while Juan went outside with Miguel to look at some of his sheep and his small garden where he was trying to coax a few vegetables from the semi-arid and rocky ground. When they had gone Maria showed Marlene her kitchen with its simple, home-made cooking range and the open oven where she baked her bread. Marlene's heart was happy. She tried to tell Maria in what little Spanish she knew how she, too, would like such a kitchen and the simple, outdoor life of the mountains. But Maria shook her head wisely, and answered, so far as Marlene could gather:

"For you, a fine house with Juan. It is right it should be so."

She showed Marlene, too, the small room where Juan had slept as a boy and where he still slept when he came to visit them. Maria said many things concerning Juan which Marlene could not understand, her knowledge of the language being, as yet, rather limited. But she sensed there was still some mystery about him she did not understand.

Darkness was falling by the time they said goodbye to the old couple. Juan looked happy and relaxed, and Marlene guessed he must have spent a most happy childhood.

"Whenever life palls or I find myself becoming tired and irritable I come up here," Juan said as they drove away. "Now, of course, I shall have you—heaven be praised."

"But you'll still visit them, of course."

"Oh yes. For as long as they both live. They saved my life. When they found me I was terrified and at the point of death from starvation and exposure."

"But how on earth did that come about?" she asked him. "And what happened to your own parents?"

At this he stopped the car and turned to her. "These are the things I wanted to tell you, my reason for bringing you up here. I do not tell many people. There is no point. Many times I have asked Miguel and Maria to come and live with me, or to come to Blanes for a holiday. But always they smile but shake their heads and say 'no, my son'. They are people of the mountains and would not be happy down in the valleys."

"That I can well understand. Up here, it's a world apart, so peaceful and uplifting."

She almost laughed aloud when she recalled, fleetingly, Ramon's speculation of Juan having a woman up here. She waited for Juan to tell her about his real parents. But first he reached for her coat from the back of the car and put the rug across her knees, and as he talked to her the stars came out one by one, brilliant in the clear mountain air.

"It is a sad story," he told her, his arm about her shoulders. "My parents were in this country on holiday. They were driving through the mountains. My father was a man who always liked to explore untrodden paths, and I remember we became lost and settled down to camp for the night. I still shudder at the memory. Both my parents were killed—murdered by a gang of brigands for their money and the food we had with us. Somehow I managed to escape, to outrun them and hide."

"Oh, Juan—" Marlene exclaimed with horror, "how terrible for you! How you must have suffered!"

She flung her arms about his neck and kissed him, anguished that he should have suffered so much so young.

He smoothed her hair and held her close to him and went on with his story.

"I don't know how many days I wandered about. All I can remember is the hunger and the cold nights. The brigands took everything. The tent, food, the car —everything. Days later when I lay ill and too weak from lack of food even to move, Miguel found me when he was rounding up a stray sheep. For weeks I was ill—delirious. They could speak no English and I could speak only a very little Spanish."

The significance of what he was saying suddenly dawned upon her.

"You—you mean your parents were *English*—were here on holiday from England?" she asked in astonishment.

He laughed softly and kissed her. "That's right. When I asked you to marry me I cheated a little in still allowing you to think I was Spanish."

"Juan, how could you?" she said indignantly. "But why?"

He ran his fingers down her cheek caressingly. "Forgive me. I wanted to test you, to see if you would marry me even though I was not of your country and you might be subject to our rather narrow conventions. You see? I forget most of the time that I am not a born Spaniard. I said 'our conventions', not theirs. Oh, my darling, I adore you. You were willing to marry me no matter what my nationality or under what restricted conditions."

"And what shall we be when we're married?" she queried. "English or Spanish?"

"We shall live a married life like any other normal English couple. Just as long as you're happy, you can stay at home, carry on with your career—anything you fancy. Am I forgiven?"

"You're forgiven. But did you never trace any other relatives? Grandparents, for instance?"

"In time, yes. But as you saw, Miguel and Maria were poor sheep farmers. When Miguel found me I was in a very critical state. I was dying of starvation and exposure, I had a fever, and for a long time I could remember nothing except my name, which was John. They interpreted it as Juan, and that I have been ever since. Up here, they saw no newspapers. If my parents and I were missed, Miguel and Maria had no way of knowing. They had obviously crossed from England by car and were touring and camping. Winter descended, and by the time the spring came I had come to love Miguel and Maria so much, I had no wish to leave them. It was a good many years later that I came across an old English newspaper reporting my parents and myself as missing."

"So your real name is not Montserrat?"

He shook his head. "It means literally, John of the saw-tooth mountain. Juan of Montserrat—which is what I was to Miguel and Maria. When I began to grow up Miguel gave me a gentle push in the direction of Barcelona where I went into hotel work—and now here I am, to cut a long story short."

"Did you make any attempt to trace your relatives?" asked Marlene.

"Not for a long time. I was too busy. When I was not working at my job I was making good the gaps in my education, reading avidly anything I could get hold of. When I had enough money saved I bought my first hotel and gradually added to their number. All of this kept me busy, too, and it was not until February of this year that I made what might be called a pilgrimage to the place where I was born."

"And you found your people?"

"Yes. But it grows colder up here. We will proceed on our journey and talk more when we arrive home."

How he found his way back along all the narrow, twisting, unmade roads back to the main Barcelona road Marlene could not think.

"Every week, except in midwinter, I visited Miguel and Maria," he told her. "It is little wonder that police never found Miguel's house, but I would know the way blindfold."

They spoke little on the journey back to Blanes. Marlene was thinking over all Juan had told her, admiring him still more for the way he had educated himself and made his way so well in a strange country.

"What about something to eat?" Juan said as they got out of the car at the Hotel Marina. "You must be near starving by now."

"Not really, but I must admit that mountain air has given me an appetite. Don't let's go into the staff dining room, though. Let's have an easy meal in my flat. We shall not be interrupted there. That is, if you're not afraid of what the staff might think."

He put his arm about her waist. "I shall make our

engagement known at once, you can depend upon it, and we shall be married just as soon as possible."

He sought out Micaela and asked her to take soup and cold meats with fruit and cheese to Marlene's flat. The girl's dark eyes opened wide on hearing it was a meal for two, but when Juan told her they were to be married, her pleasure was spontaneous.

"I tell the others?" she asked, clasping her hands together excitedly.

Juan smiled. "Tell as many people as you like, Micaela."

When they reached the privacy of the flat Juan took Marlene in his arms, declaring his love for her over and over again, only releasing her when Micaela came into the room with their meal set out on a trolley. She had also brought up a bottle of wine, and Juan told her that on no account were they to be disturbed again.

It was a meal Marlene would never forget as long as she lived. She had never felt so happy in the whole of her life. The simple meal was like a banquet, the wine like nectar. Juan waited until they had finished eating before he told her the rest of his story.

"Who are your family, then, Juan?" she asked him.

"The Hetheringtons."

She sat bolt upright and stared at him in puzzled amazement. "The Hetheringtons! You—you don't mean the family of Lord Hetherington I used to work for—Roger's family?"

"The same."

"But—but I don't understand. Are you absolutely sure, Juan?"

"I'll show you. Excuse me a moment."

He went to his room and a few minutes later returned with old newspapers over twenty years old printed in England and showing photographs of an eight-year-old boy and his parents. The father was so like Juan as almost to be himself. A faint memory began to stir in Marlene's mind—the story her father had told her about John Hetherington and his wife and child being murdered, years ago, and in the mountains of Spain.

"But this must mean you're the—the heir to the Hetherington estate?"

"That's right. I have my birth certificate, copies of those of my parents—everything."

"Then—then why—"

He laughed at her incredulous expression. "Why have I not claimed my heritage? I was far more interested in something else. You. I came to the Hetherington estate that day to look around—after having some talk with various local people—to see what kind of place it was and, if possible, have a word with some of the family incognito. Then, still without having announced who I was, I met you. Darling, as soon as I saw you something happened to me. I suppose it must have been love at first sight."

She gazed at him in wondrous delight. "Ever since then? I—I can't believe it!"

He nodded and looked tenderly into her eyes. "Nevertheless, it's true, my darling. But I guessed there was some unhappiness in your life as well as the death of your father, and I did not want to rush you. Then, horror upon horrors, Ramon seemed to be winning you."

She shook her head vehemently. "Never! Not even before I knew I loved you. But there was something else between you and Ramon, wasn't there?"

He nodded. "Didn't I tell you? We were both once in love with the same woman. I didn't want that to happen again. *Was* he in love with you?"

"I don't think so."

191

"I suspect he commandeered you simply to annoy me."

"Perhaps." She wondered whether to tell him about Ramon's conspiracy on Frasquita's behalf, but decided not to. Then Juan said:

"There was a time when I thought you were avoiding me, giving me the cold shoulder for Ramon."

She smiled. "I thought you were in love with Frasquita."

"Frasquita? Whatever gave you that idea?"

But she shook her head. "People in love imagine all kinds of things."

At this he kissed her, and it was a little time before conversation was resumed. Then Marlene asked him:

"Darling, what are you going to do about being heir to the Hetherington estate?"

"Nothing—unless you wish it. I'm quite happy here. More than happy now that I have you. But what about you?"

She smiled and rested her head on his shoulder. "Whatever you want to do and wherever you want to be is good enough for me. I fell in love with Juan de Montserrat, not John Hetherington, but I bless the day—that dull, foggy February day when you found me."

He gathered her to him. "So do I, my darling, so do I. Now winter has gone and in our hearts it will be summer always."